LONG POINT

Stories From the East End

SHELBY RAEBECK

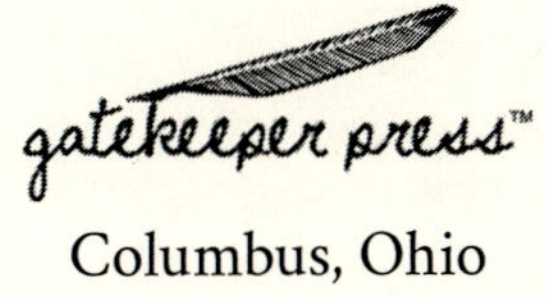

Columbus, Ohio

Louse Point: Stories From the East End (2nd Edition)

Although many of the settings in this collection represent actual places, the stories told are entirely fictional. All characters are products of the author's imagination and any similarities to actual persons, living or dead, are entirely coincidental.

The following stories first appeared in other publications:

"Dream Girls" in *Mid-American Review*; "Promised Land" (as "Horses") in *The East Hampton Star*; "Freetown" (as "Trapped") in *Sudden Flash Youth*; "Frankie's World" (as "Whisk Me Away") in *Walrus*

ISBN (paperback): 9781662917820

Cover design by Enterline Design; photograph by Shelby Raebeck

Published by Gatekeeper Press
2167 Stringtown Rd, Suite 109
Columbus, OH 43123-2989
www.GatekeeperPress.com

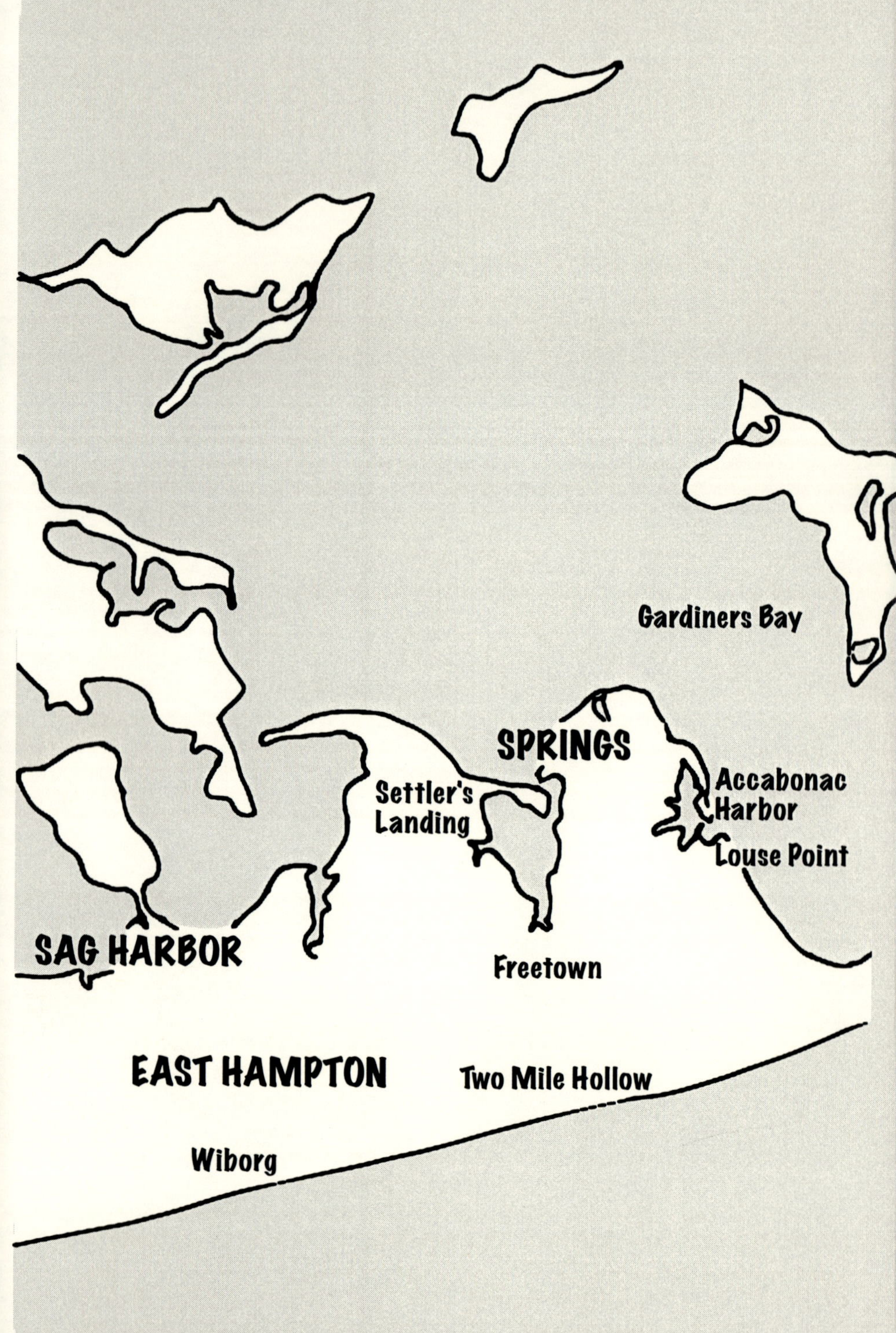
Gardiners Bay
SPRINGS
Accabonac Harbor
Settler's Landing
Louse Point
SAG HARBOR
Freetown
EAST HAMPTON
Two Mile Hollow
Wiborg

THE EAST END

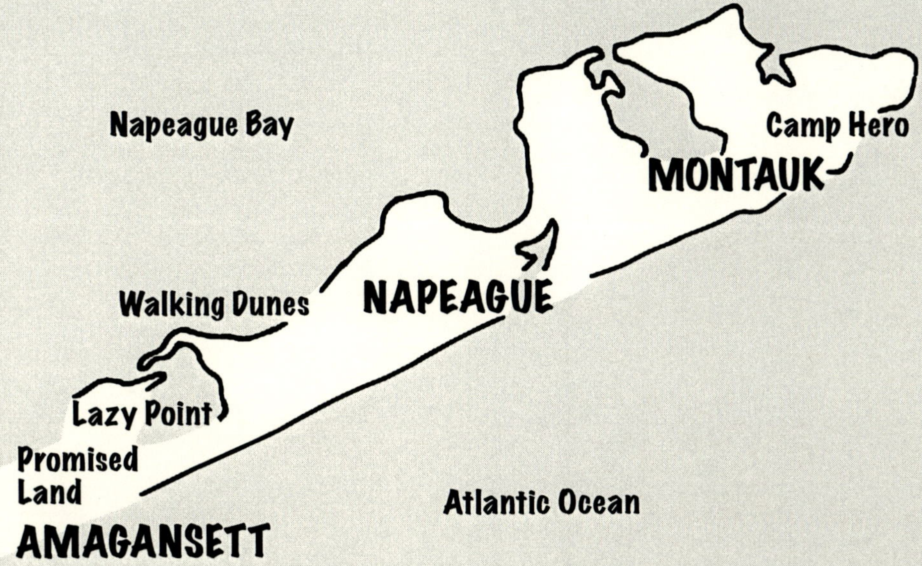
Napeague Bay
Camp Hero
MONTAUK
Walking Dunes
NAPEAGUE
Lazy Point
Promised Land
AMAGANSETT
Atlantic Ocean

Contents

Dream Girls

I wake intermittently to the distant scraping sounds of my father in the basement patching the foundation, but remain in bed on the second floor until finally, near noon, my sense of obligation yields to the weightless comfort of doing nothing. At which point, I rise from bed effortlessly, wander down the hall, and stop at the back stairs to gaze into the sun-filled bathroom. Rid of all compunction, I linger in the doorway and study the shafts of white light beaming through the upper pane of glass, and watch the translucent curtains hanging before the lower half, which is open. The curtains flutter lightly, then surge into the room, swelling and splitting apart, as if around an entering body.

As my father and I sit at the dinner table before covered bowls of fried chicken and vegetables waiting for my older sister, Lonnie, who dances at a club called "Dream Girls," he bows his head, closes his eyes, and whispers a long prayer. When he glances up at me his eyes clench, the skin around them scrunching into deep creases as if I'm too bright to look at. He doesn't speak, just squints at me, and when he closes his eyes to resume his prayer his face relaxes and the creases open out into thin gray scars, tributaries that have run dry.

The last time I saw water run through those lines was just over a year ago on my mother's birthday, six days after she died. The three of us were sitting in the back yard where Lonnie was playing guitar and singing. Newly retired, my father wore sunglasses and as Lonnie sang "Happy birthday dear Mother" I watched him mouth her name, Carla, as tears slid out from behind the shields of dark glass into the thin grooves that curved around the cheekbones.

When Lonnie finished, he grabbed his knees and hoisted himself onto his feet, wiped his eyes with a handkerchief and strolled off to begin repairing the house. Lonnie sat there looking around the yard, shifting leaden eyes from spot to spot. Then she stood up, her eyes still searching. "Well," she said, "I'm not gonna just sit here," and she too walked off, taking the first job she found.

I remained in the back yard for a long time unable to get up from my chair, as if I were part of a tableau that would be destroyed if I left. More than anything, I suppose, it was a sense of balance that kept me from following my father and sister, a sense that the past simply wasn't done yet.

"You know," my father says, eyes opening and quickly clenching, "while you're hanging around feeling sorry for yourself, there's plenty of work to be done."

"I'm not feeling sorry for myself," I say, and before he can insist I am, Lonnie bursts into the room, the wind from her body fluttering a strand of my father's grey hair into his face, which he fingers to the side. As she flops into her chair, my father blinks slowly, maintaining his thought.

"You could help out in the garden," he says.

"Yeah," Lonnie says, lifting the top from the bowl of chicken and stabbing a thigh, "get some dirt on your hands."

"Help yourself," I say.

"Thank you," she says.

My father shakes his head and exhales. Then he lowers his forehead and moves it back and forth in his fingers as if the endless sarcasm, steadily on the rise since my mother died, has finally overwhelmed him. I'm just getting up from my chair to go and comfort him when he looks up with such anguish I think he's going to be sick.

"Now where are you going?" he says.

"Nowhere," I say, settling back down.

He shoves the bowl of carrots toward me. "What are you, filled with helium?"

"Listen," Lonnie says, one cheek bulging with food, "one of you has got some explaining to do." She holds our attention with a finger while she chews and swallows. "My make-up's disappearing. First a mascara and now a lip-stick." She tears away another bite of chicken. "So?" she says, her tongue pushing the food into a cheek, "we got a queen in the house or what?"

Lonnie's ride comes to take her back to work and my father sits before the television flipping through a stack of magazines, one at a time, cover to cover, and I wander up the stairs and see a figure standing in the doorway of the bathroom silhouetted by the thick orange twilight—my mother. I am not surprised. She's wrapped in a towel and, as I walk close to see if her face has aged, she leans back, smirking, and thin spears of light pass across her eyes.

"What?" she says.

"Nothing," I say, noticing she hasn't aged.

"Well," she says, "you coming in?"

Hesitating, I look past her out the window, expecting the apparition to fade, and gaze into the darkening blue sky spreading above the fields of tall grass, and farther, down to the wide strip of cobalt sea.

"Well?" she says.

I step cautiously through the doorway and she removes the towel, revealing bra and panties, sits on the edge of the bathtub and rubs a palmful of lotion into each of her thighs, which ripple away from her fingers, then into her calves. I stroll over, lower the seat cover, and sit on the toilet. She rubs lotion along the length of her arms, walks over to the full-length mirror, and unlatches her bra.

"Mom," I say, before she releases it.

"Ricky," she says, mimicking my tone and pulling off the bra.

She takes a breast in each hand and raises it up, looking at her reflection.

"If you don't mind," I say.

She turns to me. "Embarrassed by your own mother?"

"I'm fourteen years old."

"Stop it," she says.

"I am," I say, and stand up so she can see how much I've grown, to nearly six feet.

She watches as I step closer and as her head tilts slowly back, following my approach, a shadow passes over her eyes—my shadow. I have stepped between her and the window and she seems to be weakening.

"Mom?"

The flesh on her face has suddenly grown worn and tired. She tries to smile but fails.

"How old did you say?" she says.

"Forget it."

"No, no," she says, "tell me."

"Mother, forget it."

I step back from the window and point to the mirror and she follows my finger and again sees her gleaming reflection. She glances cautiously back and I nod to reassure her, and she returns her eyes to the image. Slowly, her hands slide up her stomach, move over her breasts, and knead the soft flesh in her fingers.

She looks at me and smiles, her eyes sparkling. "You're still mine, aren't you?" she says, blinking slowly and dislodging two tears that roll off her cheeks into the dying sunlight.

The next day I descend at lunch time and find Lonnie standing before a crackling frying pan in a mini-skirt and high heels, a spatula cocked over her shoulder.

"Day shift?" I say, sitting at the table.

"No," she says, "I'm going to the beach."

"Jesus. Sorry for asking."

"Did you use up my shampoo?" she says, pivoting back to face me, her eyes rimmed in black, lips a glossy pink.

"I don't take showers in the summer," I say.

She turns back to the stove. "There must be a ghost," she mutters.

"Maybe there is," I say. "The ghost of Mom."

"Ricky, for Chrissakes. Let go."

"I'm not holding on."

Lonnie sets out the hamburger with a thick slice of tomato and a small dish of mayonnaise and sits across the table, staring past me out the window. She places a napkin on her lap, lifts the burger in her finger tips, and takes a bite baring both rows of teeth, careful not to smudge her lipstick. She slowly chews and swallows, still staring, and as she sinks deeper into thought, her eyebrows squeeze down toward her nose, nearly joining. She lifts the burger and takes another snarling bite.

"Lonnie," I say.

But she doesn't respond, just keeps staring.

Then she glances down at her watch. Then at me.

"You say something?" she says.

"What were you thinking?"

"Wouldn't you like to know."

"That's why I asked."

As she gazes at me, her forehead unfurrows and her eye-brows float apart. "Actually," she says, "there's this other dancer, Doreen. I told her about you."

"Yeah?"

Lonnie stands up. "Yeah," she says, and opens the door, not looking back.

The kitchen door sucks closed behind Lonnie and I take a bite of the hamburger, which smells of her musky perfume, and throw the rest away. In the stillness I hear my father working below, scraping the cement from the wheel barrow and pasting it on the wall, holding a steady mechanical rhythm, a trowel-full at a time, scraping it up and pasting it on . . . and I head off to the beach.

When I wake from a nap the sun has begun its descent and I see a gold barrette blinking from the hair of a girl standing by the water. I'm trying to think of an excuse to approach her when I feel a thin stream of sand on the back of my neck. I roll over and see Crisco. He bends to the side, folding his bad arm and leg together, the left side of his body contorted from cerebral palsy, and drops down beside me.

"So," he says, eyeing the girl, "you make a move?"

"Naa."

Crisco lifts a small sand cake and heaves it at a soda can. "Well," he says, "are you going to?"

Without answering, I stand up and walk cockily toward the girl who's at the edge of the surf, but just as I reach her she turns around and I lower my eyes and pass on by. With nowhere else to go, I dive in the icy ocean and force myself to stay in until I can no longer feel my feet. On my way out, I try to walk normal and the girl offers a smile, but I can't tell if it's friendly or mocking.

"Water's nice," I say. "Not cold at all."

"You kidding?" she says. "It's freezing."

"No, really, it's warm."

"Well, you won't catch me in there."

"Actually," I say, feeling myself going too far but unable to stop, "it might be too warm."

This time she doesn't respond, just peers at me as if I've moved off to a great distance, and I wander back to Crisco.

"So," he says, "she gonna bear your children?"

"Naa," I say.

He puts on his glasses and lofts a sand cake at my leg. "She live out here?"

"Didn't ask."

"Jesus Christ, did you get her name?"

"Nope."

Crisco struggles to his feet and paces in a circle, his whole body dipping with each step on his bad leg. "Goddammit, Ricky," he says, "we're supposed to be screwing these girls."

"So you go over there," I say.

"Me?" he says. "Shit." And he folds himself back down and pours sand from one hand to the other.

We sit there for a long time, sifting the sand, lofting an occasional sand bomb, our shadows slowly lengthening.

Finally, I stand up. "I'm outta here," I say.

Crisco looks up at me, squinting into the low sun. "She's still there," he says.

I shake my head. "I can't Crisco, okay?"

When I'm several paces away Crisco calls my name and I turn back. He tosses a sand bomb straight up in the air, lets it burst on his head, leaving a small pyramid, and sits there grinning at me.

"Maybe tomorrow," I say, and walk slowly home.

From the doorway to the family room I see Lonnie hovering over my sitting father.

"At least have the guts to face the truth," Lonnie says.

"I'm talking about common decency," my father says softly.

"Fine. Then I won't ask anything of anybody. Ever."

I walk in and sit in the easy chair. My father blinks slowly and looks at me.

"What I'm saying applies to you as well," he says.

"I got arrested," Lonnie says.

"From now on," he says, still looking at me, "you only get back from this place what you put into it."

"What'd she do?"

"They raided the club," Lonnie says. "Busted all the minors."

My father keeps looking at me. "Your mother would be devastated."

"Maybe not," I say. "I mean, maybe it'd make her feel good to see Lonnie needs her."

"No, no," he says, "your mother wasn't selfish, never for a moment."

"Jesus Christ," Lonnie says, "will you two kindly get on with your lives?"

Still looking at me, my father shrugs and I shrug back.

We hear the thumping bass of Lonnie's friends pulling in the driveway. The horn honks and Lonnie rushes from the room, then pokes her head back in.

"Ricky" she says, "maybe you should come."

"I don't know," I say, feeling too young. "Probably not a good idea."

"Idea?" she says, withdrawing from the doorway, her voice trailing away toward the kitchen. "Since when is having fun an idea?"

The kitchen door thumps closed and as the motor and music fade away, my father's gaze drifts out the window to where the sunset has been pressed by cloud cover into a fiery slit along the horizon, and he begins softly humming. I watch as the features on his face fade beneath the gathering darkness, and listen to him hum, over and over, the same simple melody.

In the morning the bathroom door is closed, with light pushing out around the edges. I lean close to the door and hear cosmetics clinking against porcelain.

"Are you dressed?" I call.

My mother laughs. "Yes," she says, "you have nothing to worry about."

I walk in, see her leaning over the sink looking in the mirror, and stroll over and sit on the cast iron radiator.

"So fill me in," she says. "What's going on around here?"

I tell her Dad's repairing the foundation and that Lonnie's got a vegetable garden but spends most of her time either dancing at the club or running amok with her low-life friends.

"And you?" she says, applying mascara in short measured arcs.

"I'm doing fine," I say. She turns back from the mirror and raises her eyebrows. "I am," I say, "honest." She smiles and tilts her head to the side. "What?" I say.

"Ricky, I'm your mother."

"So?"

"So, talk to me."

"Lonnie keeps telling me to let go of you."

"Then let go," she says, smiling at me and dabbing her cheeks with rouge.

I don't answer and she steps over and touches my jaw with her finger tips. "Don't think so much," she says. "Just do what you feel."

"I feel like letting go."

She runs her fingers through my hair, her finger nails tracing thin lines along my scalp.

"Mother," I say.

"Relax," she says, gazing dreamily at her hand in my hair.

"Maybe you're the one who needs to let go," I say.

"Why?" she whispers, kissing me on the forehead. "Why do I need to let go?"

"Because you're—" I begin, but stop myself, as if it would be my saying it that would make it true.

She withdraws her hand from my hair and looks away. "Go ahead," she says, "say it." But I don't respond and she looks back at me, her eyes again hopeful. "In that case . . . " she says, turning away and removing the towel.

But seeing the back of her naked body triggers the words. "Because you're dead," I say.

She hangs the towel on a hook and turns back to face me. "How can you say that?" she says, her hands floating helplessly out to the sides. "I mean, look at me."

It takes all my strength to stare back into her dark, pleading eyes and ignore the smooth flesh of her hanging breasts, the mild puff of her belly, protruding like a small pillow.

"But you are," I say. "Dead and gone."

When I get to the beach the same girl is lying on her towel reading and I spend the whole afternoon waiting for Crisco to arrive and coax me into trying again. But he never shows and when the girl leaves, she walks right past me without looking and I feel myself bursting with frustration and set off for a long run, not turning back until I reach the thin stretch where the ocean and bay nearly push together. When I return my heart is thumping, sweat streaming down the center of my chest, and I dive in the ocean, which doesn't even feel cold. I dive again and pull myself along the dark bottom, and when I burst up out of the water and look at the empty beach, I feel this intense longing for the girl. "You see," I want to shout to her on the shore, "it's not cold. You see? I was telling the truth!"

Back home, Lonnie's sitting in the shadowy late-afternoon kitchen sipping coffee. I sit across the room where I can see the white v of her panties.

"I'm a man and I want you," I say.

"Stop it," she says, frowning and crossing her legs.

"What's wrong?"

"There's no fucking hot water, that's what."

"So?"

"So, I'm supposed to go out tonight."

"Go for a run first, generate your own heat."

"Believe me," she says, "it's generated." After a minute she adds, "What's with you anyway? You meet a girl?"

"Nope."

She steps over and jabs me in the stomach. “Come on, Ricky.”

“I swear.”

“A guy?”

“Nobody.”

“Alright then,” she says, and walks off, stopping at the doorway. “But Ricky,” she says, turning back.

“Yeah?”

She gazes at me a moment, scrutinizing, then shakes her head.

“What?” I say.

“Nothing. But you should have come last night. Doreen asked about you.”

“What about tonight?”

“Tonight?” she says absently, already thinking about something else. “I’ll let you know.” And she saunters off toward her room.

“Lonnie?” I call.

Getting no response, I release a long pent-up stream of air, lay my head on the table, and stretch my arms out to either side.

My father walks in and opens the refrigerator. “All that work finally get to you?” he says.

“You know,” I say, lifting myself with great effort onto my elbows, “not working can be as hard as working.”

“Is that so?”

“Like the monks in Tibet,” I say. “You don’t see them out pulling weeds.”

“Who says you don’t?”

"Anyway," I say, "I think it might be a good idea to take a break from my, you know, my—"

"Hiatus?"

"Yeah," I say, lifting myself onto my feet.

"Well, you can start by helping me put up the screens."

"Now?" I say, hoping he'll say tomorrow, not wanting the transition to be too abrupt.

"Now," he says.

I head up to my room, softening my steps as I pass the bathroom, then stop and listen. Hearing nothing, I step over, push open the door, and find the room empty, the sink clear of cosmetics, the tub completely dry.

The screens are wood-framed and heavy and have to be hung on the outside or tacked on with nails where the hooks have rusted off. My father goes back in the house to hold the screens from within and I climb to the top of the ladder and look off at the gnarled pink clouds, motionless over the ocean. The wind has ceased for the day.

Meanwhile, my father is kneeling on the floor of my bedroom holding the screen in place, waiting for me to tack in the nails. I tap one into the corner of the window frame then give it a whack and it bends, so I try another, and this one falls out. As I tap in a third I notice a white form looming behind my father, but force myself to concentrate on the nail. When I get it in, I tap one in the next corner.

Over my father's shoulder, I see my mother in a white gown leaning toward the window.

"Ricky?" she whispers.

I shake my head, avoiding her eyes.

"Ricky," she whispers. "I'm still here."

I again shake my head and mouth the words, "Mother, no."

My mother sighs and kneels down beside my father, her body growing diaphanous, brown eyes and brown hair blending with the dusky air. Gazing at the side of his face, she slowly reaches a hand out and runs the backs of her fingers along his jaw. She begins to whisper to him and his eyes, gazing past me into the twilight, glimmer faintly with the sky's fading pink light.

"Dad," I say softly, "what are you thinking?"

"Ricky," my mother whispers harshly, keeping her eyes on my father.

"Huh, Dad?" I say to him, "what?"

He blinks slowly. "Your mother," he says.

"You miss her?"

"Sure," he says. "Sure I do."

I watch his eyes swell with pink-tinted water. "That's it?" I say.

He releases a long stream of air, his brow pressing down over his eyes. "I was always working," he says.

"That's not what I remember," I say.

My mother points a finger at me. "Stop it," she whispers.

But I concentrate on my father's squinting face, peering past me into the sky.

"I remember you starting to work after she got sick," I say. "I remember her getting more and more frantic and you just trying to keep busy."

"She wanted to be loved," he says. "That's all."

"But you did," I say.

"Not enough," he says.

I glance at my mother who raises her eyebrows at me, hoping that will settle it.

I don't know what to say, knowing I need evidence but not having any. "You love me enough," I say.

He blinks slowly. "Maybe," he says, "but women need more."

"I need more too."

I watch the water again well in his eyes as he slowly turns his head and gazes toward my mother. When he speaks, his whole face contracts, as if the rising words are too large for his throat. "You always had this, this—" he releases the screen, which I pin in place with my forearm, and lifts his hands as if out of a thick, heavy liquid—"this craving."

My mother rises to a stand, her face drawn with fear, darkness filling the hollows of her cheeks, and begins to retreat before his gaze. When she reaches the bed she slumps down onto it, as the white of her gown and the white of her flesh slowly dissipate, replaced by the settling gloom.

"I had to start working," he says, turning back to me with wide, vacant eyes. "It was like she wanted to take me with her."

"Maybe she still does," I say.

My father continues to peer at me, vaguely, as if looking through me to something else, until finally his eyes tighten, the pupils constricting into small points, and he sees me.

For a long moment we just look at each other.

A car pulls in the driveway as I tack in the last nail, and on her way out Lonnie stops directly beneath the ladder and tilts her head back, the darkness settling around her eyes. “Time to be a dream-girl,” she says.

My father offers a nod and a soft smile she doesn’t see.

“Knock ‘em dead,” I say, and Lonnie stands there gazing up at us through the diminishing twilight.

“I’ll see you boys later,” she says finally, walking out from beneath the ladder. “Don’t wait up!”

Lonnie enters the waiting car, which backs out of the driveway and roars off toward town, and again the only sound is the gentle washing of the ocean.

It’s almost too dark to see as I send the hammer down a final time, and when I look up my mother too is gone, my father holding the screen, gazing past me toward the sea. I turn around, settling myself down on the top rung, and watch the dark lines of waves pulsing toward shore, a single filament of light blinking from crest to crest.

WALKING DUNES

Despite the building boom and snarled July traffic, Darlene was pleased to see the town pond just as she remembered it.

"Look," she said to her daughter, Sydney, strapped into the seat behind her, "they've still got the two swans."

"They're not the same ones," Sydney said. Sydney was fifteen and tired of riding in the back, where she'd been since they'd left Tucson four days earlier.

"It's the *idea* that's the same," Darlene said.

Darlene had been doing that throughout the trip, reminiscing about the early days with her husband, Frank, on Long Island's East End, then steeling herself for the mission that lay before her—going there to find him and bring him back to Tucson.

They entered the village of East Hampton and turned into the parking lot behind the row of high-end boutiques. Darlene parked in the sun and held the back door open for Sydney.

"It's too hot," Sydney said, slowly straightening and texting her brother, Wilson, three years older, who was supposed to be meeting them. "I can barely breathe."

"It's the humidity," Darlene said. "But then you have the ocean."

"Wilson's not answering," Sydney said. "All I know is it's a deli on Main Street."

"Isn't that his jeep?" Darlene asked. She pointed at a red jeep a row away with Arizona license plates.

On summer break from ASU, Wilson had left for Long Island two weeks earlier to track down his father, who had left a week before Wilson. Eight days after leaving, Wilson had called home to say he'd found him and Darlene had packed Sydney and their sleeping bags into the car and headed east.

The two women walked down an alley and turned onto the sidewalk running along Main Street. An A-frame placard listed the day's specials for the Atlantic Deli. Sydney led her mother inside and to the back where two young men sat at a counter, one of them Wilson, wearing wrap-around sunglasses, no shirt, and long paisley shorts that covered his knees.

"You found it," he said.

"This place was always here," Darlene said.

She and Frank had met when she'd come east on vacation with a friend's family and had come back a week later and stayed two years with him in Montauk.

"What's that?" Darlene pointed at the plastic cup of greenish fluid before Wilson.

"Smoothie," he answered. "Green Vibrance."

"It's too hot for that stuff," Darlene said.

"Too humid," Sydney corrected.

"The heat's why you drink it," Wilson said. "Tons of electrolytes."

Darlene lifted the cup and took a swallow. "Tastes like river water," she said.

"Bet they didn't have these," Sydney said.

"Come on outside," Darlene said to Wilson.

Wilson gave a complicated, four-step handshake to his friend and followed his mother and sister out to the sidewalk.

"You got here fast," Wilson said.

"We drove thirteen hours a day," Sydney said. "Slept in the car."

"So where is he?" Darlene said.

"Fishing," Wilson said. "Joined a boat called the Riptide."

"Day trips or overnighters?"

"Don't know. I got a job my first day here, running the cabanas and equipment shack at Main Beach."

"You got any money?" Darlene said.

"You can't take his money, Mom," Sydney said.

"How much you got?" Darlene said to Wilson.

"Forty bucks."

"Give me thirty." She looked at Sydney. "He'll get it back," she said.

Shaking his head, Wilson removed a billfold from his pocket and peeled off thirty dollars.

"I'll call you," Darlene said. "Or Sydney will." She turned to leave and saw Sydney drifting the other way, toward the ice cream parlor next door.

Darlene turned back to Wilson, running her eyes down the length of his body, from sunglasses to flip-flops. "Aren't you just Mr. Chillbody," she said, more proud than sarcastic.

Wilson shuffled his feet.

"Don't forget why we came," Darlene said, and she turned back to Sydney, who stood gazing through the parlor's open door. "Chop chop, Missy," Darlene called. "We're going to Montauk."

With Sydney again strapped in behind her—Darlene's older sister had been killed as a teenager riding in the passenger seat—they joined the line of cars headed out to the island's eastern tip.

"Down that road," Darlene said, pointing to the left, "they've got these huge sand dunes. And this great spot your father and I would go with a bottle of wine and watch the sun set over the bay."

They drove up onto the bluffs and could see the ocean on one side and the bay on the other, then descended into the village of Montauk with its string of cinder block motels and gift shops. Once through town, they turned and headed toward the fishing docks.

They parked in a gravel lot and walked along the harbor until they found a vacant slip with a sign for the Riptide. A small blackboard attached to a piling had the words "Due back at 7PM" scrawled across it, and Darlene led Sydney into a bar called Rex and ordered two Cokes.

Sydney texted someone, then slipped her phone in a pocket and sipped her drink. "What if he's not on the boat?" Sydney said. "What if he already went to the next place?"

"Going back' has always meant Montauk," Darlene said.

"What was Utah?"

"That was 'taking a break.' You remember that?"

"Kind of."

Darlene turned and gazed at Sydney. "We were living in Needles," Darlene said, "where your father went to truck mechanic school." She took a sip of her drink and made a face, surprised at the syrupy sweetness. "He finished the course and worked as a mechanic for about a year. I used to think how great it was, him coming home all gunky, getting himself smack into something. Then one night he says, 'I need a break,' lifts his jacket from the hook, and walks out. Only that time he called from where he went."

"Salt Lake City," Sydney said.

"So the three of us packed up and moved to Utah."

"And you loved it there."

"I *learned* to love it there," Darlene said. "Love is something you learn."

They heard the groaning horn of an approaching vessel, Sydney swallowing the last of her coke, and walked out to see a sixty foot white trawler lumbering into the harbor. Two men on deck prepared the ropes for mooring but not Frank. Once the boat had tied in, three more men appeared, two of them joining the first two to help haul sacks of fish across a wide plank onto the dock. Darlene approached the one who wasn't hauling.

"This your boat?" she asked.

"No," the man answered. He had a thin, drawn face with a spray of freckles across his forehead. "I'm the captain."

"I'm looking for Frank Barrett. I'm his wife."

"Not here," the captain said. "Why you hunting him?"

"He's got a family," Darlene said.

The man glanced at Sydney leaning against a piling, then turned back to Darlene. "Check the Cedar Hills Cabins," he said. "On the right side just before you get back to the village. Hey," he said as Darlene turned to walk off, "you get tired of chasing, come on back and I'll buy you a steak dinner."

"I don't get tired," Darlene said, "but thank you."

At the entrance to Cedar Hills Cabins, Darlene slowed but didn't stop. "I want to show you the spot," she said. "Sun's about to set."

They passed back through the village, past the scenic view, and turned onto the narrow gravel road Darlene had pointed out earlier.

The road dead-ended at the bay and a sign beside a trailhead explained that "Walking Dunes" referred to the ever-shifting nature of the huge sand dunes that lay in the path of the northwest wind off the bay. Beyond the sign, they could see sandy peaks, partially covered in beach grass.

"So these are different dunes than when you guys were here," Sydney said.

"They could walk all the way to China," Darlene said, "but they'd still be the same dunes."

"Are you going to make him come back to Arizona?" Sydney asked.

Darlene pulled in a deep breath and started the car. "That's where our home is," she said, exhaling and backing up.

The sun was just setting when they pulled into the Cedar Hills Cabins parking lot. Darlene spotted a black pickup in the far corner, pulled up behind it and saw its Arizona tags.

"You stay here," Darlene said to Sydney. She knocked on the cabin door closest to the pickup, standing slightly to the side away from the window next to the door. She knocked a second time.

The door opened and her husband first saw the car idling behind his truck, blocking any possible exit.

"Hello Frank," Darlene said, stepping into view.

"Darlene."

"Everything okay?" Darlene asked.

"I'm okay," Frank said.

"You sure made us come a long way, Frank."

"That Sydney in there?" Frank peered over at the station wagon then called out, "That you, Sydney?"

A muffled, "Hi Daddy," came from the car.

"Poor girl just drove clear across the country with no money for hotels," Darlene said. "Go over to her, Frank. Ask her how she likes Montauk."

"I'll do it," Frank said. "Then I'm going back inside."

"No, Frank. After you ask, you've got to listen to her answer."

Frank walked over to the car and Sydney opened her door, hugging her father without getting out.

"How you liking Montauk?" Frank said.

"I'd like it more if I could do something."

"Like what?" Frank said.

"Like go get something to eat."

"I got some chips inside."

Frank walked back into the cabin and returned with a bag of tortilla chips and a small container of French onion dip.

"I love you, baby," he said to Sydney, then walked back into the cabin.

Darlene followed him. The cabin consisted of one wood-paneled room with a kitchenette on one side and a door to a bathroom on the other. No lights were on and it was getting dark. Frank sat back on the sofa, locking hands behind head, closing his eyes.

Darlene stepped over and opened the small refrigerator, no higher than her chest. Inside she saw a carton of lemonade and a loaf of bread.

"How long you been fishing?" she asked.

"Nine, ten days," Frank said.

"You gone back to the house?"

"I drove by the first day. It's been all redone. Hardly recognized it."

Frank's father had been a Montauk fisherman nearly his entire life. Frank had joined him his first year after high school, had a falling out, and headed west. They eventually made up, the old man sending Frank money during a couple of dry spells, but Frank had only seen him one more time.

"You think fishing is going to bring him back?"

"No, I do not, Darlene."

"Then what are you trying to prove?"

"That's your way of putting it. Everything's about proving something."

"When you walk off, Frank, your family doesn't just disappear. We're still there. Only one of us is missing."

Frank sucked in a deep breath and closed his eyes.

"I'm taking Sydney out to get something to eat," Darlene said. "If you want, you can come. If not, we'll be back in an hour."

"Darlene," Frank said, stopping her at the doorway. "You don't have to do this."

Darlene peered back at him. "Oh no?" she said. "If I don't, who will?"

Darlene drove Sydney in silence to Iguana, a Mexican take-out in town with a row of two-person tables on the sidewalk. They each sat with a combination plate and ate beneath a streetlamp, a steady flow of summer visitors strolling past.

"You sure got quiet," Sydney said.

"Just thinking," Darlene said.

"About Daddy?"

"About the summer carnival they used to have right here on Main Street."

"About Daddy," Sydney said.

"There were these two policemen," Darlene said, gazing down the street, "a husband and wife couple, and they would collect stuffed animals and attach them to their belts."

"What if you didn't chase him?" Sydney said. "Wouldn't he eventually come back?"

Darlene looked at Sydney, taking a moment to focus. "I waited two full months before packing us up and moving to Utah," she said. "And when we finally got there, he barely recognized us."

"Was he drinking?"

"He'd been sober a full year by Utah. But he was having migraines. When he goes off, he doesn't go to raise hell, he just goes. And he starts forgetting."

"I would just let him go," Sydney said. "And let him forget."

"You say that. But being forgotten is a terrible thing."

"By somebody who's still there it is," Sydney said. "But not by somebody who's gone anyway."

"Cause then you're forgetting them too, right?"

"I guess."

"And you know what happens when you forget someone?" Darlene said. "When you forget someone whose blood you've got in you? The little place in your heart where they lived, it dies."

"Not if you fill it with something new," Sydney said.

"You ever try and fill a milk carton with orange juice? Doesn't matter how many times you wash it out, the orange juice doesn't taste right. Same thing with daddies."

A middle aged couple walking past with a small dog made an effort, both man and woman, to make eye contact and offer a smile, first to Darlene, then to Sydney. Darlene smiled back but Sydney's effort was more of a wince.

"They think it's nice," Darlene said, "a mother and daughter eating outside on a summer evening."

"It is nice," Sydney said. "To finally get a respite from that damn car."

"What do you know about a respite?"

"SAT word. One of Miss Dauber's 'Crucial Two Hundred.'" Darlene had taken cash advances off credit cards to send, first Wilson and now Sydney, to SAT prep class on Saturdays.

"Memorizing them is one thing," Darlene said, her eyes sparkling with admiration, or more precisely, recognition—though Darlene had never gone to college she had had stretches in high school when her teachers had gushed with praise—"but actually using them? That's downright uppity."

"Pretentious," Sydney said.

"Good one," Darlene said. "Supercilious."

"Supercilious," Sydney recited. "Coolly superior; haughty."

Darlene looked across the table at Sydney, bit her lip and nodded, and asked the waitress for the check.

They pulled up behind Frank's pickup, so close they nudged the truck's bumper, and Darlene shut off the engine. No light was visible in the cabin.

Darlene went to the rear of the station wagon, raised the door, and removed their sleeping bags and pillows.

"Here," she said, pushing one of each through Sydney's window, and turning to see Frank.

"Sydney can take the sofa-bed," Frank said, "but the two of us will have to find spots on the floor."

"It's better you finish this up on your own," Darlene said. "Get it all done with. We'll be fine out here."

Frank returned to the cabin and Darlene settled herself in the front passenger's seat, and she and Sydney tucked and twisted until finding positions that permitted sleep.

Darlene awoke at dawn to tapping fingernails on her window.

"I gotta go fish," Frank said.

Darlene glanced back at Sydney curled up in the back seat, turned the key to accessory and lowered her window. "How do I know you're coming back?" she whispered.

"Come on, Darlene," Frank said.

"I got to know," Darlene said, and she quietly slipped from the car and walked into the unlocked cabin, Frank following.

She located Frank's empty duffel bag on the floor and, in the bathroom, his shaving bag, in which she could see the electric razor she'd bought him for Father's Day a month earlier.

"How's the new razor working?" she asked him.

"Fine," he said.

Frank was obsessive about having smooth skin, shaving twice, sometimes three times a day when he was able. He could wear the same jeans six days in a row, some days didn't even bother to shower, but he would never leave his razor behind.

"What time's the boat coming back?" she asked him.

"Later tonight. We're fishing bass off Block Island, about twenty miles out."

Darlene walked out to the car and, closing the door gently behind her, backed out of Frank's path. Sydney stirred and went back to sleep.

After they had each showered in the cabin, Darlene and Sydney drove back to East Hampton and on to Main Beach, where, not having a parking permit, Darlene pulled into a handicapped spot beside the boardwalk that led to the clubhouse and cabanas.

Inside a small office with an open-air window they found Wilson, a wad of keys dangling from a lanyard around his neck as he scribbled something on a pad.

"You got a girlfriend out here?" Darlene asked, before he'd even looked up.

"Hey," Wilson said. "You find Dad?"

"Yes," Darlene said. "You got a girlfriend, a lease, a contract for your job—any commitments at all?"

Wilson turned his attention to Sydney. "What's up, Syd? You guys having any fun, or is Mom too busy tracking the bad guy?"

"We're all going back to Arizona tomorrow," Darlene said.

"Who's going back?" Sydney said.

"All of us."

"Wo now," Wilson said. "I'm making sixteen bucks an hour. And I've got a place. In fact, I was thinking maybe you guys could stay with me for a couple of days. Just have to check with my housemates."

"We came out here to get your father," Darlene said. "The job's not finished till we're all back home."

"My part was finding him," Wilson said. "And on top of that, I loaned you money."

"I know I owe you," Darlene said sternly. "The point is, we owe each other. That's how families work."

"Mutual servitude," Sydney said. "Nice."

"Right now, you need to put family first," Darlene said.

"Right now," Wilson said, "I need to save some money so when I get to school I can eat." Wilson was majoring in Outdoor Recreation. His grades had never been high like Sydney's but he had always managed. And the fact was, he was paying, and borrowing, for college himself.

"You can't make him, Mom," Sydney said.

"I'm not *making* him," Darlene said. "I'm asking for help. That's all I've ever done—ask for a little help."

Wilson and Sydney exchanged a look. "Let me see what I can do," Wilson said.

"We'll meet you in the morning," Darlene said.

"Let me see," he said.

Darlene and Sydney got back to the car just before the lot attendant pulled up on her Vespa, and they drove into the village of East Hampton. Darlene found a parking space on Main Street, sat still a while, then shifted the rear view mirror to look at Sydney.

"Every year," she said, "I would plan this trip back east for the four of us. And every year, there would be a reason we couldn't go."

"Can we do some shopping?" Sydney asked.

"Absolutely," Darlene said.

They joined the crowds on the sidewalk, bought ice cream cones, and made their way to a Manhattan haberdasher, where Darlene withdrew her credit card and bought Sydney a floppy hat with a pink ribbon, Sydney admiring herself in the storefront windows as they walked back to the car.

When the Riptide ambled into the harbor at 10:15 that evening, Darlene and Sydney were waiting in the station wagon a hundred yards or so from the slip. They watched the crew unload the fish and waited till Frank had walked to his pickup and driven off. Then Darlene got out and approached the captain.

"That's Frank's daughter there," Darlene said, pointing back to the station wagon in which they could see Sydney's hat-clad figure. "Frank is heading home in the morning and needs the money he's owed."

"He gets paid on Fridays," the captain said.

"We've got to drive back to Arizona with our two children. This all just came up. She—" Darlene again gestured toward Sydney—"has a brother in East Hampton that came out here to find Frank."

"Frank know you're here?" the captain asked.

"Here in Montauk or here talking to you?"

"Both."

"Yes to Montauk, no to talking to you."

The captain eyed Darlene another moment. Then he removed a roll of bills from his pocket. "You're lucky I'm carrying," he said. "I can give you the four days' wages but not the commission."

He handed Darlene four hundred dollars. Darlene extended her hand and shook the captain's.

"If he shows up for work tomorrow, I'll keep him on the crew," the captain said. "But I won't pay him twice."

Darlene pulled into the Cedar Hills parking lot, up close behind Frank's pickup. She shut off the car and sat still, thinking, Sydney watching from the back seat.

"Wait here," Darlene said.

She knocked once and entered the cabin. Frank was sitting on the sofa typing into his laptop. He maintained a steady correspondence with several people from the AA chapter he'd joined in Utah. Darlene sat in a vinyl chair opposite him.

"Sydney and I are going to sleep in the parking lot again tonight," Darlene said. "Wilson should be back at his house packing up. In the morning we're all going home."

Frank closed his laptop. "Not me," he said.

"You got two kids waiting on you, Frank."

"They're here because you forced them," Frank said.

"Wilson came on his own. To help save his family."

"It's an idea you're talking about, Darlene. *Your* idea. The family is what it is."

"And what's that, Frank? A mother and two children driving four days to find their father? You call that a family?"

"I call that *our* family." Frank watched her a moment. "The running away part is fucked up. I can admit that, Darlene. But it's the chasing that causes the agony."

"I'm not chasing, Frank," Darlene said, her voice tightening. "I'm holding on. I'm *saving*."

"Saving an idea," he said.

Just then the cabin door creaked opened. Wilson poked in his head, then entered, followed by Sydney.

"Hey Dad," he said, and he and Sydney walked over to stand beside the sofa, facing Darlene. "I can't get back the deposit on my place," he said.

"Try again in the morning," Darlene said.

"I can earn more money staying here," Wilson said.

"Wilson," Darlene said, "don't do this."

"This isn't about me, Mom."

"It's about all of us," Darlene said.

"It's not about me," Sydney said. "I didn't want to come, Mom. You know that."

"Darlene, listen to them." Frank stood up, walked around the sofa, past the kids to the rear of the room. Darlene had always thought his giving ground signaled a need for her to step forward. But now Wilson and Sydney stood there in the space between them.

"Don't you want a father?" she said.

Wilson hoisted a thumb back over his shoulder. "He's right there."

Darlene pulled Frank's pay from her pocket. "Listen," she said, her hands beginning to tremble as she flipped through the bills, "there's enough here for a couple of nights in nice hotels."

"That's your pay, Daddy," Sydney said.

"We'll find places with pools," Darlene said. "And internet in the rooms," she said to Frank.

Darlene looked from Frank standing in the dim light at the rear of the room to her two children standing before her.

"Please," Darlene said. "It'll be the trip we never took."

Somewhere on I-81 in Virginia, Darlene lifted her cell phone, already silenced, and shut off the power, canceling the temptation to check and see if anyone had called. Sydney too had decided to stay behind, Wilson assuring Darlene that his room was big enough for two, Frank promising to drive over to East Hampton every day off to check on her, and by the time Darlene left the next morning, the three of them had already headed off to Main Beach to see about getting Sydney a job.

Darlene drove straight through to a Motel Six outside Knoxville, the second night stopping at one near Dallas.

The third morning, she didn't wake until nearly ten o'clock, despite the fact she'd picked up two hours switching time zones, and packed up her things in a hurry. She needed to get home to regroup, get her bearings, and it felt urgent that she reach the house while it was still light.

Darlene drove hard through the day, holding the small wagon at eighty. But when she crossed into Arizona, still nearly two hundred miles from home, the sun had already set, and she pulled into an empty rest area as the last of the day's light drained into the horizon.

Darlene got out of the car and stood in the warm breeze blowing in off the desert. She walked from the parking area across the sidewalk and picked her way through the sage and piñon, the rush of the highway softening behind her. Stopping where she could no longer see the parking area, she gazed up at the first few stars, seeing more as the sky darkened and her eyes adjusted.

Darlene lowered herself to the ground, heard something scurry away, and lay on her back, the heat from the earth warming her body, her unburdened feet humming with the absence of weight.

Darlene lay there on the desert floor gazing out at what was now a broad sheet of stars, letting the earth take her where it would.

Trophies

When my big brother, Willie, and I were in high school in the mid-90s, living out back in the tool shed we'd fixed up, most nights Willie would hang out at our neighbor Rudolph's house, smoking pot, cranking Traffic, Led Zeppelin. A Vietnam vet, Rudolph had inherited the house from his mother, and during the warmer months when the windows, one on each side, would be open, I'd hear the thumping music from Rudolph's through one and our parents' voices droning endlessly back and forth through the other.

One night, I moseyed over and found Willie and Rudolph deep in a sofa, smoking a bone to "Freedom Rider," and Willie asked me if I wanted to see a thumb.

Rudolph lifted himself up, walked over to a glass-enclosed cabinet and removed a small red metal lock box, returned to the sofa, rotated the tiny notched dials until the lid popped open.

"There she is," Rudolph said.

I sat beside him, got a whiff of the same preservative they'd used for the frogs in high school, and saw in the box, lying on a cotton bed, what looked to be a small toy soldier, like the nutcracker our mom hung on the Christmas tree, only flesh-toned, unclothed, its oval of face flat and smooth with a satiny varnish.

"When you kill a dude," Rudolph said, "you can either spend your life wishing it didn't happen or take a piece of him. People think it's sick. But sometimes being sick is the only way out."

Wasn't till '08 that Willie came back to the East End, flying in from Sacramento on the red-eye, arriving at JFK at five-thirty, which meant I had to leave my basement studio in East Hampton at three.

"Still liking Sac City?" I asked as we worked our way back through the morning rush on the Belt Parkway.

"It's got everything I need," Willie said.

I'd flown to Sacramento a couple years earlier when a girlfriend had moved out and Willie had violated a restraining order, sleeping in his car in front of her apartment, then flew out again a month later to help him get going, driving him to the supermarket, the harness races at Cal Expo where I had to confiscate his wallet and send him in with a twenty, a couple interviews for bartending jobs.

We exited the Parkway onto Sunrise Highway, morning traffic thinning as we headed east.

Willie'd only agreed to come back to Long Island because I'd hit my own stretch of bad luck, the trenching company I worked for letting me go for the quiet winter months but then not rehiring me in March, and had talked him into fixing up and selling the Settler's Landing house that had been sitting empty since our mother had died nine years earlier.

We passed the "Bridgehampton, Settled in 1656" sign, ambled through the canopy of maples lining Main Street, drove on to the pond, and entered East Hampton.

Willie and I had worked together as carpenters, after I finished high school and Willie bailed on his three-month attempt at the Merchant Marine Academy, having learned the basics from our pops who'd been a handyman at one of these monster East Hampton estates.

"How'd you get off work?" I asked.

"Told the manager my mother died."

"You mention when?" I said.

"Doesn't matter," Willie said. "Sacramento's got twenty other Outbacks, or the equivalent, within a ten mile radius, all chock full of thirsty motherfuckers."

We pulled into the driveway of the home where I lived just outside the village, continued around back to a worn spot beside the bilco doors that served as my entrance.

Willie opened his door but didn't get out. "You understand this isn't some kind of Dorian Brothers redo," he said.

"I hear you, bro," I said. "Wam bam. Fix her up and get her sold."

Coffee in hand, Willie gazed past the Settler's Landing house into the woods, the silver sheet of Northwest Harbor visible beyond the stalks of oak trees.

"Damn shame," he said.

Two months into his attempt at the Academy, our father had had a heart attack and stroke, one right after the other, and the day of the funeral our mother sold, basically donated, the twelve-acre preserve adjacent to the house, bought with an inheritance she'd received out of the blue from a grandfather she'd never met, to the East End Land Conservancy. She'd always said she wanted to be in a position to make a difference.

We levered up a window, popping the latch, and climbed in, the place dusty but tidy, a few spider webs, pictures in place on the walls. Willie opened the pantry door, shelves still lined with cans, Mason jars of rice and flour, stepped in and reached up to the top shelf, taking down our father's 12-gauge shotgun.

Till that moment, I'd never known where my dad kept the gun, though on two separate occasions, I'd woken in the middle of the night and, seeing Willie's bed empty, had walked to the house and seen through the window Willie sitting in the living room, rifle across his thighs as if on guard, to keep people out or keep them in, I couldn't tell.

Willie grabbed two shells from the top shelf, loaded the gun, kneeled down and took aim out the window we'd climbed through, panned side to side looking for a target, then withdrew the rifle with a sigh and returned it to the shelf.

We headed out through the kitchen door, strapped on tool belts, and began ripping away the worn planks of the porch and steps, rusted nail heads tearing off shanks. Two hours later, the old porch lay in a pile beside the driveway, and we measured, marked off the new porch along the house, tacked on tarpaper and flashing.

I drove to town to pick up lunch, and we took a game trail down to the strand of seaweed-strewn shore, narrow even at low tide, sat on a couple of big rocks and each ate a banana and half a bologna sandwich.

Out over the harbor, a bird flew in lazy figure eights, then angled toward us, its size apparent as it neared, larger than a gull or raven, dropped down some sort of air chute, curving to within a hundred feet of us, and we saw it was larger than a hawk or even an osprey.

"Bald eagle," Willie said.

"I heard some chatter about them coming back," I said.

The eagle circled us, Willie raising himself to a stand, holding his sandwich behind his hip. "What the hell you looking at?" he yelled.

The eagle flapped its massive wings hard, one time, and sailed back out over the water.

"Bird's going to come back and kick your ass," I said.

"Oh yeah?" Willie said.

"Yeah," I said, stepping over to where the sand met the woods to take a leak.

Willie moved up beside me, hooked a hand on the back of my neck. This was how it'd always been, Willie coming up on me, trying to get a rise.

In high school, he'd gotten into fist fights with every bad-ass in town, after which the other guy would always breathlessly explain to whoever would listen that Willie was crazy, didn't feel pain, that even if you got him down, he wouldn't tap out, like it wasn't a fight but a fight to the death. But as the little brother, I'd always seen him from the leeward side.

"You're an asshole," I said to him, and leisurely finished my pee.

We fetched the post-hole digger and wheelbarrow from the truck and dug holes, mixed cement, and set six posts for the deck, 300 feet of cedar decking, charged to Willie's credit card, scheduled for delivery next morning.

Willie checked the last post for plumb and leaned the level against the house.

"Not bad," I said.

"What's not?"

"You and me back on Settler's Landing."

"The fuck it isn't," Willie said.

Willie had left Long Island Christmas day thirteen years earlier when, a little more than a year after our dad died, Willie and me moving back into the house, working together banging nails, my mother found him in the garret over the garage with a neighbor who lived two doors down, a widow twenty years older, the two of them lying amongst the garbage bags of clothes Mom'd been collecting but never delivering to Goodwill. When Willie packed up and drove off that afternoon, it wasn't because our mother'd demanded it—more because she hadn't.

"Sorry dude," Willie had said to me when I stopped him in the driveway, "this mistake needs to find a new habitat."

By late afternoon the second day, we'd laid the deck, which ran half the length of the house, installed the railing and slats, and framed out the porch roof, Willie surprising me with the suggestion that we construct a gable and eave above the steps, rather than a much simpler flat, shed-style roof. "Whatever we spend, we'll get back double," he said.

We stashed the tools in our old living quarters out back and, returning to the truck, stopped to admire our work.

"Good call on the eave," I said.

"Remember how she used to tell Dad she wanted a porch she could sit on?" Willie said.

"'With company,'" I said.

"'Sit out with company and watch the wide world.'"

"We hook up the heat and electric, you could move in," I said.

"I've got a place."

"What's with the hard-on for Sacramento?"

"It's not here, that's what."

"There's a lot of places that aren't here."

"But only one Sacramento."

We stopped at Bo Peep, the only year-round tavern in town. When the bartender, an older guy with a comb-over, delivered our drinks, Willie lifted and eye-balled his glass.

"Really?" he said. "A summer pour in May?"

"What's that?" the bartender said.

Willie lowered his glass to the bar. "Make it a double," he said.

The drink came, and Willie took a sip, gazing into the mirror opposite, and sighed. "This is why I don't come back," he said.

"You just have to drink a couple at home before going out," I said.

"No," Willie said, pushing his jaw at an angle toward the mirror, "cause of that fuckwad."

In the mirror, at the other end of the bar, sat the director of the land agency our mother had sold the twelve acres to.

"Wasn't like he forced her to sell it," I said.

"Just presented the *opportunity,*" Willie said.

"Made her feel good," I said, "saving the planet."

"She didn't save shit," Willie said.

I drained the last of my beer and told Willie I needed to go, next day being Saturday, my day to have breakfast at the Highway Diner where a group of women came every week after their morning spin class. I liked to show up well rested.

"Couple of 'em bound to be single," I said.

"It's the married ones are less choosy," Willie said.

"Not what I'm looking for," I said.

"What you're looking for you can't have," Willie said. "The lonelier they get, the higher they raise the bar."

"They could raise it to the moon," I said. "I'd still clear it."

"Then why aren't you married?"

"You just said, married ones aren't choosy," I said. "I got standards, Jack."

"Well well," said a voice at my shoulder. The director of the land agency. "What brings you back to town?" he said to Willie, who watched him in the mirror.

"I had to fly in some cheap labor to fix up the house on Settler's Landing," I said, extending a hand.

The guy shifted toward me, his face not quite aligned, but pleasant. "You're the little brother," he said, taking my hand. "I'm Mike."

"Hey Mike."

"You guys selling the house or moving in?"

"Donating it to charity," Willie said, turning back from the mirror.

"Yep," I said, "we're giving it away."

"You know," Mike said, "the Wildlife Federation's been tracking the bald eagles, looking to set up a visitor center. Settler's Landing is a prime nesting site."

"We had a run-in with one this afternoon," I said.

"An eagle?"

I looked at Willie, then back at Mike. "It came for our lunch so we fucked it up."

"Eagles have federal protection," Mike said.

"Our lunch has local protection," Willie said.

"You shot it?" Mike said.

"Worse," I said, "we *yelled* at it."

"Told it there was a new sheriff in town," Willie said, "and he better watch his ass."

"Got it," Mike said with an airy chuckle, backing up a step, nodding, returning to his chair at the other end of the bar.

Next day, after breakfast at the diner, I picked up Willie. He didn't ask so I didn't give a report.

We were installing new headers over sagging windows when a red Cherokee came curving up the drive, a guy with wire-rimmed glasses and purple fleece emerging, saying he was with the New York State Wildlife Federation, telling us two pairs of Bald Eagles had nested on Settler's, the Federation monitoring their chicks that had recently fledged.

"We're also keeping tabs on the terns and plovers," he said, glancing toward the harbor.

Willie gave me a look, unimpressed, returned to hand-sawing two-by-fours, and the dude and I stepped away from the noise where he told me that with board approval the Wildlife Federation could offer up to ten percent above appraised value, pay cash to save time and paperwork, and best of all, we'd be helping save the living heartbeat of the American wilderness.

"Where'd you get this?" I said, reaching over to his waist to feel the fleece.

He smiled at me, unsure. "Just say the word, and I'll order an appraisal."

"Online?" I said. "Or you pay a zillion dollars in the village?"

"Online," he said.

"Figured. Well," I said, holding out a hand to either side, "at least we've got this."

"It's a special place," he said, shuffling his feet.

"Come back tomorrow," I said. "I'll talk to my brother."

At Bo Peep, a chick in white shirt and bowtie served us drafts, and Willie handed her his card.

"That thing must be getting heavy," I said.

"Be out of here soon enough."

"I'm thinking Smoky Mountains," I said.

"What's there?" Willie asked.

"Everything you got in Sacramento, only cheaper."

"They got dry heat in the summer?"

"Better," I said. "*Wet* heat."

"They got the Sierra Nevada on one side, Pacific Ocean on the other, wine country right down the road?"

"They got all the rot-gut you want," I said, taking a gulp of beer, "and big muddy lakes you can swim in with your clothes on."

Mike and the Federation dude came in and took a bar table behind us. In the mirror I watched Mike hang his jacket on a chair, stand there in his green sweater vest over light blue shirt, spot us, and approach.

"Pete here says the Wildlife Federation wants to make an offer on your place," he said. "They've got some deep pockets."

"I've heard," I said.

"You got another buyer in mind?" asked Mike.

"A children's charity," Willie said.

"A hospital?" said Mike.

"A charity," I said.

"Like UNICEF?"

"Like Shriner's," I said.

"That's a hospital," Mike said.

"St. Jude's," Willie said.

"That's a hospital too."

Willie broke into a smile. "Fuck the children," he said. "What are you drinking? How about your buddy there?"

"I'll ask," Mike said, but Willie grabbed him by the elbow, holding him in place, and called the bartender.

"A round of Cosmos for my two friends," he said.

The bartender nodded, set two martini glasses on the bar, and began dumping liquids into an aluminum shaker.

"You don't have to do this," Mike said.

"Who said I did?" Willie said.

"I'm saying you *don't* have to."

"Which means somebody must think I do."

The bartender poured the pink mixture into the glasses, affixing a wedge of lime to each. Willie lifted the glasses and handed them to Mike.

"Have yourselves a party," he said.

All we had left to do was finish shingling around the repaired windows and install an outdoor lamp I'd found sitting in my landlord's garage. But as we reached the house, I realized I'd forgotten my tool belt. I dropped Willie and headed back to the apartment.

I took my time, low on energy, struggling to keep Willie's pace. I didn't get the urgency, why Willie was always so driven to get out of there—truth was, I never had—and drove along Hands Creek Road, every half mile or so eyeballing a construction site for a new house, thinking what we should do is focus in right here and build a couple of these houses ourselves.

Returning to Settler's Landing, I saw the red Cherokee in front of the house, found the kitchen door open and, going in, calling Willie's name, saw the door open to the pantry, and headed back outside.

As I walked across the newly built porch, feeling it solid beneath my feet, thinking hell yeah, we did good work, I heard the boom of the twelve-gauge.

"Asshole," I said out loud and headed to the trail.

Halfway to the water, I came across Federation Pete.

"Seen my brother?" I said.

"No," he said. "Heard a gunshot and figured I'd come back later."

"Probably kids shooting cans," I said.

"You guys discuss my offer?"

"Not yet," I said. "But we're finishing up the reno today."

"Let me know," he said, handing me a card from his wallet and continuing back to his car.

Reaching the thin strand of beach, I saw Willie a hundred yards up, crouching low, motionless, and walked toward him, wondering if maybe he'd hit pause, was declaring some sort of truce with the place.

But as I got closer, I saw he wasn't crouching but kneeling, hunched forward, supporting himself with the shotgun, puking I thought, or maybe praying, two things I'd never seen him do.

Then I saw the eagle.

Before Willie, it lay on its belly, one huge brown wing extended a good three feet, the other folded in half, poking into the air, the bird's white head cocked to the side, its eyes, yellow rims around fierce black circles, locked open.

Willie twisted his head to look at me, mouth half open, and again I thought he was going to be sick, or maybe cry out to God.

"What are you going to do now?" I asked.

Willie turned back to the eagle and, laying down the rifle, placed one hand on the bird's head, holding it against the ground, while with his other hand he fingered the buckled wing, separated a feather, and dislodged it.

"Get a shovel and bury it," Willie answered.

"Then what?"

One hand closed firmly around the feather, Willie scooped up the rifle with his other hand, stood, and took a long look at the woods and harbor.

"Sell 'em the house," he said, "and get the fuck out of here."

Lazy Point

My twin sister Kathy said phone calls only pushed people farther away, so she rode the train three hours from Amagansett to my girlfriend's studio in the East Village, flopped down in the beanbag chair and told me Mom had moved a bed and dresser up to her studio over the garage. The garret wasn't even insulated, Kathy said. Good for painting, sure, with a view of Gardner's Bay on one side and the Lazy Point marsh on the other, but not for living.

"They're barely talking," Kathy said. "Peter, you need to come."

What I need is to find a job, I thought, but this was Kathy, who never asked for anything, the type who'd sit there bleeding and wave you past to help someone else. I walked Kathy to the subway so she could catch the afternoon train back to the East End, and next morning told my girlfriend Ronnie I'd be back in a day or two, and she said sure, whatever, no doubt happy to have me off the couch, where I'd spent the last couple months between jobs, watching TV, flipping through classifieds.

I arrived at Amagansett in the mid-day July heat and walked the three miles out to Lazy Point, winding slowly around the marsh to the small house on stilts dug deep into the sand. I knocked, heard nothing, and went in. Whereas the outside of the house was ramshackle—mildewed asbestos shingles and peeling paint—the inside was clean and tidy, due to Kathy, a mason jar of lilac on the counter, the kitchen table already set for the next meal, cloth napkins folded beneath unmatching forks.

I went out to the garage, separate from the house, and took the exterior stairs to my mother's room. She had a bare-wood shelf on one side that held some folded clothes, a bed neatly made in the middle—Kathy no doubt—and an easel and small table covered with paints by the window overlooking the bay. But as I walked further into the room, I saw beyond the bed her huge gold-framed mirror lying flat on the floor, a circle busted into the center of it.

During the two years of my father's early retirement, when Kathy and I were in high school and we moved three different times, the first and third time into the same house, that mirror, a wedding gift from her grandmother, was the one and only thing Mom had personally bubble-wrapped and moved herself. Now there it sat, encircled in broken glass, a chunk of glass knocked out of its middle the size of a cannon ball.

Reggie, my father, had come out of retirement to become a court cop, but his earlier business had been insulation. Ran a decent business, only he said the asbestos was eating away his lungs, therefore the early retirement and a series of moves, from a one-story to a two-story and back to the one, Kathy and I taking over the next door neighbor's abandoned shed and installing a wood stove for our last two years of high school, Kathy taking days, sometimes weeks off from school to tend the garden she planted, minding our shed but also the main house, hanging laundry on a line strung from the gutter to a tree, cooking dinners, even on the days she went to school filling the crockpot with meat and veggies to simmer throughout the day.

Then the town board created a social services division and a special committee to help locals find jobs. There'd been two suicides and two murders within a single year, all by out-of-work fishermen, and somehow my father got on the list and this carpetbagger social worker named Teddy took up his case. When the court officer job came up, it was the first one Reggie had no reason not to take. All he had to do was pass a multiple-choice exam and a marksmanship class. "Shit," I remember him saying, "I'm gonna learn to shoot for free, then they're gonna pay me to keep order in the most orderly court in the state." Which they did, him sitting there beside the dais, clipboard and docket in hand, calling up each case, checking them off, turning out the lights at the end of the day.

I called Kathy's cell—she worked part-time as a housekeeper at the largest house on Lazy Point, the only one with a grass lawn, the rest with beach grass and sand—and asked for a ride to Town Hall. Before I walked outside to meet her, I found a plastic pitcher in the cabinet, filled it with water, and placed it in the nearly empty refrigerator, refrigerated water the closest thing to an antidote for the muggy summers of Lazy Point.

At the far end of the marsh, we passed this girl Ginger's house, and I asked Kathy to slow down. The only one-night stand I'd ever had was with Ginger, the organist at St. Luke's. Her parents, who'd run a tiny seafood shack and bar in Lazy Point, had finally given up and moved south and Ginger and her brother, Karl, had stayed on in the paid-off house, Karl, a big quiet guy who posted a neighborhood watch sign and did night patrols through the winter, this in Lazy Point, a neighborhood that in the off-season had at most six or seven inhabited homes, Karl opening the seafood shack each Memorial Day to grudgingly serve clams on the half shell and beer to summer renters and windsurfers.

I was overcome with the urge to knock on the front door—the one-night stand with Ginger occurring senior year, the night after the funeral for one of the fishermen who'd offed himself, Ginger playing long notes that were more whiney than mournful, glancing up at me in a way I thought coquettish but was more likely apologetic—just knock and walk upstairs to the room where she'd taken me after I'd driven back to the church in Reggie's truck and offered her a ride. But Ginger's house looked empty, nothing in the dirt driveway but a beagle sleeping in a patch of shade, connected by a noose to a metal flag pole, and a block further, we passed the seafood shack with its two umbrellas over two empty picnic tables.

"Whatever happened to Karl?" I asked Kathy.

"Who?" Kathy said.

"Ginger's brother. He still around?"

"Why wouldn't he be?" she said.

"What does that mean?" I said.

Kathy blinked at the road before her, and I thought back to the afternoon I'd found them together at the bay, Kathy standing by the water in a dress with puffy shoulders tossing pebbles and watching them splash, Karl sitting back on the beach, dourly looking on.

Later that night, when she came back to the shed, I thought she was drunk.

She began to undress behind the screen on her side. "I saw three shooting stars tonight," she said, her voice airy, disconnected.

I asked if she'd made a wish and she poked her head out from behind the screen. "The shooting stars *were* my wish," she said.

I don't know what it was exactly, if it went all the way back to the zygote splitting in two, me the boy half more able to venture out, get away, Kathy's half wired to stay behind, to wish and wait. But two months later it was me, not even remembering her night with Karl, who rode with Kathy on the train to Riverhead where we each paid two hundred dollars for an abortion at a clinic above a furniture store, on the return trip Kathy not letting me see her face the entire trip, gazing away from me out the window, only turning back as we reached Amagansett to tell me she was going to buy new towels and paint the bathroom with the thirty dollars she had left.

We drove out from the marsh into Amagansett, past the potato farms turned into high-end developments, the huge houses lined up like a flotilla beyond the field of flowering plants.

"Tell him to come straight home," Kathy said, "so we can fix this."

"We'll see," I said.

"Tell him," Kathy said.

I walked into the municipal building and down the hallway toward the court, passing the social services office where I saw the guy, Teddy, who had placed my father. I poked my head in the doorway, Teddy sitting at his desk in a yellow Lacoste shirt.

"Peter?" he said.

"I was wondering how things are with my dad," I said. "I've been out of touch for a while."

"Since he's been working," Teddy said, "I've hardly seen him. How about you, you got a job?"

"I live in the city," I said.

I saw this bottle on his shelf lying sideways on a little stand, inside it a green-painted dory, like the haul-seiners out here used to drop their nets in the ocean. I stepped over, picked it up, and glanced back at Teddy who was getting nervous, as if I might drop it. I fumbled the bottle in my hand, watched him tense up, then set it down and went to look for Reggie.

Through the open doorway, I saw him in the courtroom sitting one level down from the judge, one level up from a small audience of weary miscreant drivers. I sat in a chair in the waiting area, then paced the hall, until I heard the rap of the judge's gavel, and saw Reggie lock up the courtroom and followed him down the hall.

As he climbed into his pick-up, I slid in the passenger's side. Reggie glanced over at me, his expression not changing, and started the motor.

"What time you'd go to work today?" I asked.

"Same as everyday," he said. "Why?"

"I just went by the house. Where's Mom?"

"How would I know?" he said, both hands on the wheel. He had these thick-knuckled laborer's hands that didn't go with the sharp aquiline features of his face.

We drove down the Napeague Stretch and turned at the Radio Tower toward Lazy Point, passing along the marsh.

"You guys talking?" I asked.

"What's with the questions?" he said. "You should be telling me stuff. Like what you're doing in town."

"Don't worry," I said, "I'm not staying. Have you spoken with her?"

"Not the word I'd use, but yes," he said. "We're finally wrapping this thing up."

We pulled in the driveway beside Kathy's car and I followed my father through the front door.

"You bastard!" my mother screamed, and my father ducked as a glass smashed against the wall a few inches from where I stood in the doorway.

"Peter," my mother said.

But before I could respond, she was back at my father. "That mirror was an heirloom!"

"How do you know he did it?" I said.

"Did what?" my mother said. "How do *you* know what happened?"

"I went up there," I said, pointing toward the garret.

"Who else would destroy my most precious possession?" she said.

I stepped further into the room. "Well?" I said to my father.

"Could have been worse," he said.

"You bastard!" my mother shouted, firing another glass off the wall behind him.

"Dad," Kathy said, "how could you?"

I saw the hurt on Kathy's face. For a moment, we all did.

I wasn't exactly angry, more interested in hearing how he would answer her question, but Kathy just stood there waiting, and I felt I should do something, so I lunged at my father with both hands.

He shot out an arm to stop me and caught me under the chin. I grasped a handful of cheek and nose, my arms as long, maybe longer, than his, trying to squeeze him, just squeeze the shit out of him.

But he held me off with his thick hand, backing me up, choking me, till I stumbled over an ottoman.

"He didn't touch her paints," I said to Kathy from the floor, "or the easel."

"Just went for what was most precious," my mother said.

"I have nothing to do with those paints," Reggie said. "But in case you forgot, that mirror was both of ours."

"It was a wedding present from my grandmother!" my mother shouted.

"To both of us," Reggie said. "I was the one you married."

My mother shook her head, staring at him, unable to comprehend how it could mean anything to him. They each had their version, she retreating to her studio, protecting what little she'd been given, him huffing and heading off to sleep in the camper on his pick-up, siphoning off whatever extra money they had to treat his emphysema.

Kathy removed a dustpan and hand broom from the closet and walked toward the broken glass.

I sat another moment, then stood up. Reggie eyed me warily as I walked to the refrigerator and removed the plastic pitcher of water.

"I was only protecting myself," Reggie said.

Unable to find a glass, I poured the water into a coffee mug. "From me?" I said.

"You're unpredictable," he said. "Just showing up like this."

"You're the one going around breaking heirlooms," my mother said.

"Your heart ain't broke," Reggie said.

"How would you know?" my mother said.

Reggie and my mom stood there looking at each other. "Maybe I wouldn't," Reggie conceded, and he untucked his shirt from his belt and removed a sheaf of papers from his waistline.

Reggie glanced over at me and said, "That was good, though, you coming at me," then turned back and offered the papers to my mother. "Here they are," he said, "signed and notarized."

My mother rolled in her lips and breathed in deep through her nose. The broken mirror she could deal with—by firing glasses across the room, by breaking more shit—but an actual divorce. . . she took the papers.

"So this is for real," I said to Reggie.

"Yes," he said.

"Don't you have to see lawyers?" Kathy said, holding the dustpan of broken glass.

"We've done that already," my mother said. "Many times over."

"When?" Kathy said. "Why didn't I know?"

"It's not like we're never going to see each other again," my mother said.

"It might be," Reggie said. "That's the point of all this, isn't it? To give us that option."

"Then what was all the fighting for?" Kathy said. "If you're just going to give up, what was the point of all those years of fighting?"

"She's right," I said. "You can't just erase your history."

"Twenty-five years together," Kathy said, slumping onto the ottoman.

"Those twenty-five years aren't going nowhere," Reggie said. "They're just not becoming thirty."

Once Reggie'd driven off in his truck and my mother had retreated to the garret with a glass of wine, Kathy and I sat on the back deck. An osprey circled his nest at the top of the pole the town had planted in the dead center of the marsh, then landed on the perch above the nest and stood watch.

"It's good you came," Kathy said, and for a second I thought she was being sarcastic, thought it was the first sarcastic comment of her life—I sure saved the day, didn't I?—but when I looked at her, her face shone with a soft, sad gratitude.

"Their moving on might help you move on too," she said.

I called Ronnie and got her voice mail, something I *never* got, the silence a sign, no doubt. Who could blame her? I knew she couldn't wait much longer, and asked Kathy to drive me to the 9:40 train.

At the station, I told Kathy I'd call soon and climbed aboard. I took a seat half way back, resolved to take the next job I found, no matter what it was.

As the train lurched forward, I looked out the window and saw Kathy standing alone on the platform, running her eyes from window to window, unable to see through the tinted glass. I smacked a hand against the glass, but she didn't hear me, just raised her hand and blindly waved.

As the train pulled away, I stood up and rapped both open hands hard against the glass, but Kathy just stood there smiling, waving at the wrong windows.

Fremont's Farewell

PART ONE

1

First order of business today is to straighten out a rumor going around. Susan, thank you for filling me in. I have not been fired and will not be leaving the school. I have merely been placed on probation. Meaning I am being closely watched. Which I suppose I deserve. Let's face it, minions, for me, teaching has become a burlesque, an exercise in tangents, free association, blind groping—in short, an exercise in *not* teaching. Truth is, I don't give a shit, about grammar, or constructing a thesis, or even explaining the literature. Where's the joy in grammar, people? Where's the joy in explanation?

You want me to do a lesson on run-on sentences or you want to know why my wife moved out last Friday?

Oh, I waited till I was thirty-three, minions. I was sure I was ready, was sure we both were. But you have a couple of kids, they get a couple of illnesses, get diagnosed with this and that, you buy a house that needs a roof, and then a furnace, and the kid with ADHD is throwing food at you across the dinner table and the bills are piling up, and pretty soon you're not even saying goodbye when you leave in the morning. It's become a business relationship. Which to me wasn't so bad. Candle light dinners never thrilled me. And therein lies the problem. She married me hoping to convert me to a candle light kind of guy. I married her hoping to convert her to a business partner. Do not ever, my dear underlings, do not *ever* marry a project.

I did get two wonderful children out of the deal. It's just hard when she walks out, when after sixteen years of working every day to keep it together, she just walks out. They meet someone else and even if the new relationship is in fact better (and let me tell you, it rarely is, or if it is, it's because they know this time it's on them to *make* it better), giving up on something just plain sucks. All you have in life is one thing. Everybody take out a pen. Right now, everyone. If you don't have one, Hannah, borrow one. This is going to be on the final. It may be the only question on the final. All you have in life is one thing: Whatever you don't give up on. Got it? And it can't be a person, you can't hang onto tangible objects. You getting this? Look me in the eye, Charlie. You can't hang onto any *thing*—not objects, not people, not facts and figures, not your fucking grades and test scores. You can only hang onto ideas: hopes, dreams, visions. You can't hang onto a person, but you can hang onto Marriage with a capital M, or Love, or Hatred for that matter, Bitterness.

What do you have people? What do you absolutely refuse to let go of?

And what has my wife hung onto? Candle light dinners? Romance? Maybe. Maybe she has. Maybe she is now with the new guy building a life of love and decency and mutual respect. It's true, we never had those things, not really, not in any lasting way. Maybe she is, people, maybe she is . . .

Now go to fifth period. Go, all of you. Forget the damn bell. When we're done, we're done. Tomorrow we begin *Hamlet*. You think I'm self-absorbed? Tomorrow we talk about Hamlet, people, the prince of "Why me?"

2

Settle down everybody. What's going on, you all jacked up on sugar? Caffeine? Now listen, Jennifer has a question about the reading. Go ahead, Jennifer. Hmm, excellent. You are damned good at keeping us on track, Jennifer. Ok, so why does Hamlet speak so crazily, so cryptically I would say, to the lovely Ophelia? The same question we asked of Gregor Samsa when he gurgled through the door of his bedroom: is his nonsensical speaking, his retreat from reality, his devolution (I saw a band named Devolution in the East Village in the early 90s, six screaming electric guitars, no vocals, play for five hours without a break)—is his, Hamlet's, retreat from reality merely a sane response to an insane world?

Which leads to the question for today's discussion, perhaps related to Hamlet, perhaps not: "Who gives a shit?" I *am* allowed to curse, Hannah, in the context of the lesson. And even if I'm not, I'm on my way out—oh yes, their stack of evidence against me grows thicker every day—so complaining to your parents about my language isn't going to accomplish anything. You of all people, Hannah, asking about this. The rest of you getting the irony here? I've heard you down by your locker in the basement, Hannah, saying things that made my skin crawl—I heard you say you wanted to *boot-fuck Mary Whatley.* A more honest complaint, Hannah, would be that my language is too tame. Oh, I've heard you down there, Hannah, heard you say things that made me pray you would never have children.

Back to the question *du jour,* "Who gives a shit?" Come on, think. I want to know who. Your parents? You are so wholesome, Susan, it's really quite impressive. Well, maybe they do. But in what sense? What do the rest of you think? Does your parents' concern with your grades and your getting into a *good college* qualify as giving a shit? I think giving a shit implies a more genuine, less self-justifying type of concern. Okay, who else? Your friends? Maybe. As long as you're providing a buffer between them and the void—if as they free-fall through space they've got you to cling to. How about nobody? How about that? How about, you're on your fucking own. Is that better, Hannah, if I toss in an f-bomb?

Let's deal with this issue of profanity. We tell you to watch your language, then you flip on a movie or a ball game, and you hear these shining stars, belles of the ball, spewing profanity, and winning goddam awards, because it's *cinema verité*. It's realism. So why do we persist with the censorship? Is this not real—the workplace? The classroom? Why are manners so fucking important in here? Hard to know, isn't it? You're not supposed to cheat, then you see the goddamn outfielder holding up the ball like he caught it, when the replay clearly shows it short-hopped into his glove. And the guy's a fucking all-star. It's all arbitrary, minions. You can't curse when you're around adults who say you can't, but you can when you're not, and they can, and *do*, when you're not, and sometimes when you are but still say *you* can't.

The truth is, minions, cursing's a positive thing. It adds emotion, emphasis to what you're saying, and it feels damn good to boot. Because it's an expression of anger, contempt. And if you've been fucked over, you're angry . . .

Sure, it's different over in East New York where there's anger percolating at two hundred degrees, a place where you're *born* angry, than it is out here in the Hamptooooons, let alone this fancy prep school, in an English classroom. Right, Susan, Charlie, Jennifer? It depends on the context. Hannah, our resident black sheep, frothing obscene down at her locker in the basement is okay, but me up here in the classroom is wrong, is a violation of your sense of decorum. Well fuck your sense of decorum.

So yeah, I'm cursing a lot today. And I don't know, maybe it is gratuitous, maybe it isn't justified. But I'll tell you what, I've spent a hell of a lot of time hurting, if that's worth anything. One whole year, my first year teaching in Manhattan, every day after school I walked home from the west side to the east side, and before going into my shit-hole shoe-box of an apartment, I'd walk out onto the 59th Street Bridge and contemplate jumping off. Every day for an entire year. I was teaching at this fucked up school in Hell's Kitchen, and I was lonely, big-time lonely, but more than that, I was only twenty-five years old and I was *tired*. Did that year, or my best friend Danny Keymore OD'ing in my basement the night of my 15th birthday, or my mother dying when I was ten and my father not talking to me for the next five years, like he fucking blamed me, did any of that give me the right to curse? Did it give me the *need* to curse? For a lot of us, it's gratuitous, unearned, self-indulgent, it's true. But for some of us, there's an actual need. Do I qualify? Maybe. Maybe not. Is this real, people? Huh? I'm asking you: Is this shit real? How can it be, we're in a fucking classroom, right?

In the time remaining, let's get back to the question of the day, Who gives a shit? Yes, Charlie, about Hamlet. Or about Gregor Samsa, or Gatsby for that matter. We're talking Tragedy, people. Who gives a shit about Gregor's dried up bug corpse the maid takes out with the trash, or Gatsby's body floating in his swimming pool? Who gives a shit about the prince of "Why me?" Gertrude, his oversexed mother? No way. His father, the ghost? All he cares about is vengeance. Or is it justice more than vengeance? What do you think? How about you, Back Row Johnny? What if you'd been robbed of your identity, your livelihood, would you seek vengeance or justice? Would you want the perpetrator's head on a stake, or the simple assurance he would perform no such foul deed again? Either way, justice or vengeance, the ghost is committed to principle, not to people, certainly not to Hamlet, and our young prince finds himself in a nasty fix.

Why doesn't Hamlet just say fuck it, and run off with Ophelia and have a youthful roll in the grass? Because he's at that crossroads, that hellish intersection of personal desire and conscience. Because he's cursed with knowledge, people, and will never be able to mindlessly self-indulge again. Knowledge is a bitch people. No, not the shit you learn in school—not facts and names and formulas—knowledge, *the pale cast of thought.*

There, I've reduced this incredible, unwieldy soliloquy to a one-line quote, taken out and exhibited the part that served me, served my unceasing need to explain. It's what we teachers do, talk the life, *explain* the life, completely out of the literature . . . But we still have a few minutes. So who cares for Gregor Samsa, our lonely, dispossessed cockroach? Who gives a shit for Yossarian, remember him? Yes, Susan, the movie we saw, *Catch 22,* because I was too damned lazy to drag you through the book. Who gives a shit for our Danish prince?

Yes she does, Charlie, and it's exactly that fact, that Ophelia *does* care, that she *loves,* that does her in, that does our sweet Ophelia in. The prince is cursed with knowledge and Ophelia is cursed with love, and can only sing in riddles as the water pulls her under.

You see, minions, little Miss Hannah here has a potty mouth for a reason—she *knows* shit. No getting *thee* to a nunnery, eh Hannah? If you've been fucked over, you're going to say so, you're *compelled* to say so. You say fuck to counter the fucked-upness, to name it and try to keep your head above water. Ophelia sings sweet melodies, and she sinks like a stone. Not you Hannah Pottymouth. You call it what it is. Not because you're defeated, Hannah, but because you refuse to be.

That's it everybody, scram. And go ahead, curse all you want today, you proper, obedient souls. In context, out of context. Tell 'em Fremont told you to. Tell 'em it's your fucking homework.

3

Today's lesson: Catharsis. From Aristotle, people, ancient Greek empiricist. You can only know the truth from experience, people. And art, literature, said the big A, qualifies as experience, at least in his day, when they'd watch these horrifying plays, releasing their pent-up emotions—their terror and their pity, said the big A—and afterwards they'd be cleansed, healthier, better citizens. They'd watch people murder their children and fuck their mothers so that afterwards they wouldn't need to.

So how about the classroom, what do you experience in here? Is reading a book about biology or grammar or corrupt Danish royalty *experience*? Yes, Susan, but are you experiencing biology, or are you merely experiencing school, reading a book *about* biology? Once again, I'm asking you, Is this shit real?

So here's a poem a kid wrote my last year of teaching in New York City in '98. Open your English packets to page 35. I want to see if a bunch of white kids in the Hamptons can relate.

Yes, Jennifer, page 35, "Fuck the S-A-T." Really, Jennifer, offended? We're reading the language of the oppressed, Jennifer, seeking some high-brow catharsis. Your parents pride themselves on being able to say how forward thinking our school is. A couple of F-bombs shouldn't be a concern.

Now everybody together, "Fuck the S-A-T" by Cory Johnson:

Went to school with all the rest
Wasn't easy climbing out them sheets
But Mamma told me nothing good would come
Spending my life on the streets

Saw my old man standing on the corner
Didn't even know I was his
He and his boys with their same old stories
Soda pop lost its fizz

Fuck the S-A-T, uh huh
Fuck the S-A-T

Walked into that big old warehouse
First day of the eleventh grade
Security guards scurrying 'round
Wanted to spray 'em with a can of RAID

Mr. Dingle assigned an essay
Asked how may books we'd read
Miss Loudmouth told us trigonometry
Was the key to getting ahead

Fuck the S-A-T, uh huh
Fuck the S-A-T

For six solid months I packed my books
Like a mule totin' his load
Got me some Cs, got me some Bs
Counselor told me I was on the road

You gonna do good, counselor said
Separate yourself from the rest
All you gotta do, counselor said
Score high on that aptitude test

Fuck the S-A-T uh huh
Fuck the S-A-T
Fuck the S-A-T uh huh
Fuck the S-A-T

Not bad, not bad. For a bunch of pampered preps, you actually started sounding like you meant it. Feels good, doesn't it? Fight the power, right?

Perhaps you find the language disturbing, Jennifer, not because it's gratuitous, as you say, but because it's just the opposite, necessary. We need to expel the toxins, Jennifer, expel them from our minds just as we do from our bodies. Expel them any way we can.

Now all of you get out of here, the bell's about to ring. Tonight finish Act II of *Hamlet*. Now there's a boy ain't taking no SAT.

4

I was thinking last night—yes, the ex again taking the kids, the endlessly forgiving little angels, no matter what she does, what I do.... blood thicker than water, minions, much thicker—and I was thinking back to the 59th Street Bridge and New York City and I thought about Cory Johnson who was in his sixth foster home—did I tell you this?—and how the last one had burned down and he'd been caught inside and was left with a mass of scar tissue on his face, and how they'd finally scheduled cosmetic surgery for him the same week I was let go.

Stop it with your moon eyes and silence oozing with sympathy. As soon as the sentimentality starts, people, grab your wallets, somebody is trying to rip you off. Oooooh, the brave orphan enduring torment and the calloused teacher who is made to feel again. What a load of horse shit.

No, Charlie, sentimentality is the *opposite* of catharsis. It's a shortcut, achieving a result without earning it. Dunking a basketball off a trampoline. Being accepted to Bryn Mawr as a legacy. Sex with a streetwalker. A diet of simple carbs that makes you fat.

So anyway, I nominated Cory's poem, "Fuck the S-A-T," for a poetry contest. Citywide contest, one poem per school, our department chair asking teachers for nominations.

Meanwhile, another student, the darling of the English department, ambitious, hard-working, a real adult pleaser, worked with her AP teacher to construct, word by word, verse by verse, before school, after school, a long convoluted, Keatsian ode to sacrifice and service, and that's the poem the English department sent off to the contest.

Cory took the news well, focusing instead on his upcoming surgery. I did not take it so well. And Friday afternoon, staring down from the 59th Street Bridge at the black river below, I turned back and walked to the English chair's apartment on Second Avenue.

He buzzed me up and I sat in his living room and told him he didn't know shit about poetry, authenticity, truth. I never mentioned Cory or the contest, but I guess he put two and two together, and he just sat there and let me call him an egghead and a charlatan, saying only, once I had finished, that perhaps I was right, he had been unable to publish a single poem beyond his high school literary magazine.

I remember thinking, What the hell does *that* have to do with it? It's not about publishing, it's about reading, it's about *listening.*

The next day, I got called into the principal's office and was told I was being let go. And I had that shitty feeling in my gut. You know the one, Hannah, the one I've had much of my life, the ole, "You fucked up again, Ronny," only this time I'd had no choice. "Fuck the S-A-T" or some long-winded Keatsian ode? Give me a fucking break. And yes, there was a woman—there's always a woman—with whom my relationship had run its course. Oh, what a war I had with Suzy from Santa Cruzy.

Anyway, they let me go and the next afternoon I went to the hospital, was Cory's first visitor after his surgery. He asked me if the surgery had been a success but I couldn't see anything through the bandages, and I sat by his bed, the sun slanting through the blinds, and as the room grew dim, I found myself in that strange place teachers sometimes go. On the cusp of becoming more than a teacher, becoming a caregiver, an intimate, and I recoiled.

As I finally got up to leave, Cory knew I would not be coming back, knew it before I did. He said, "Thanks for coming, Mr. Fremont, it means a lot to me," and he was already forgiving me. And it's that grace, that ability to want more while accepting less, really *accepting* it, that I envy and admire and know I will never come close to having.

5

Okay, the first poem for today, the dated, antiquated "Minerver Cheevy" by EA Robinson, occasionally taught to 7th graders because it's all rhymey and sing-songy, though just like that other middle school standard, Frost's "Stopping by Woods on a Snowy Evening," way the hell over their heads. "Minerver Cheevy, child of scorn, grew lean while he assailed the seasons. He wept that he was ever born, and he had reasons." Time marches on people, steams ahead, and you can either ride the crest of the wave (what's that 3 metaphors in one sentence? Charlie, keep track if you don't mind), or you get plowed under (we're up to four, Charlie).

Take Back Row Johnny, our single scholarship student. Wait, you hear that? An audible gasp when I singled out Johnny for receiving financial aid—you actually gasped. You feel bad for him, not because he's on scholarship, not because his father's a fisherman, member of a failing industry, but because I'm saying it out loud.

Old Johnny, slouching in the back row, shuffling through the day, watching the world move on without him. "Miniver Cheevy, born too late, scratched his head and kept on thinking." I knew your father Johnny, went to school with him at East Hampton High, and he was a lot like you, maybe a bit more reckless, a bit more proud—back then being a fisherman was still a worthy calling, with a community that depended on you, and laws that protected the fish from the goddam tourists.

Don't be ashamed of needing a boost, Johnny, needing a little help—it's not easy to betray your own family, even if, *especially* if, they're the ones asking you to, sending you off to this private school, filling out financial aid applications—*can you please give us money so that our child can forsake his heritage?* No, giving up on something after so long, as some wise man once said, just plain sucks. Oh, it was me that said that, Susan? Not a wise man, but a what, Hannah, a wise what? Takes one to know one, eh Hannah?

So what's your heritage, people? Charlie? Jennifer? What are you holding on to? What are you unwilling, unable, to let go of?

Maybe, Johnny, you *should* be ashamed—what choice do you really have? You are now a card-carrying citizen in a world that doesn't give a damn for heritage, a world in which what survives is what is most ruthless, most uncaring, the cockroach, the tourist, following their natural inclinations, the merciless ocean, rising and falling, rising and falling, with you or without you.

And so we come in our circuitous way to the other assigned poem, "The Second Coming," in which William Butler Yeats addressed this very idea: "The best lack all conviction while the worst are full of passionate intensity." Don't mistake your achievement for virtue people. Your unbroken string of A's, Jennifer, your tireless upward climb—no, Charlie, I'm not saying it's bad, and your defending Jennifer might actually be good, I'll give you that, because she's only doing what she thinks she ought—but your upward climb, Jennifer, your knocking off personal goals one at a time like so many targets at a shooting gallery… If Charlie is right, and you are to be admired, Jennifer, it's not because of ambition or achievement or *conquest*—what gives you virtue is the fact that you are the helpless plaything of forces so much more powerful than yourself. The same forces that are driving the fishermen into extinction. No, *you* are not destroying them, but you are riding the wave that is. Not intentionally, *helplessly*. Just like the rest of us.

The Bible says the meek shall inherit the earth. But old Mr. Yeats wasn't so sure. After witnessing what surely seemed to be Armageddon, World War One, he placed his money on the ruthless, the greedy, the soul-less. "And what rough beast, it's hour come round at last, slouches toward Bethlehem to be born?"

Your homework tonight, minions, in honor of the two poets discussed today, the tortured E.A. Robinson, who used his initials because he was too racked with self-loathing to use his name, and William Butler Yeats, half-hearted Irish Nationalist, Mussolini supporter, who four times over the span of thirty years had his offer of marriage scorned by the same woman—four times, minnies, what does that tell you? Shame, people. The fuel for great writing is shame.

Your assignment for tonight then? None. Except for you, Johnny. Your assignment is to go home and write a poem. Because you might be the only person in here that can.

6

Happy Monday morning everyone. God, you look like zombies. Let's try this, you sleepy souls, let's crank some Irish rock 'n roll. Susan, YouTube Boomtown Rats' "I Don't Like Mondays." Plug your laptop into the projector; find a version with lyrics. Now crank it up. All together, everybody: *Tell me why, I don't like Mondays, Tell me why, I don't like Mondays, Tell me why, I don't like Mondays, I want to shoo-ooo-ooo-ooot the whole day down.*

Yeah, baby. Sing about shooting a bunch of people dead, that ought to wake your catatonic asses up.

Today, my captives, I would like to do a lesson on synonyms. My son calls them cinnamons. Last week, we both stayed home two days from school—how was the sub, minnies? Mrs. Frosty Nips? Tried to learn your asses some punctuation, did she? Well good. Anyway, we took two days, played ball in the yard, walked into town for ice cream cones. It was amazing to walk into the village during the school day, seeing the workaday world, a bit disorienting at first, you feel like you're not supposed to be there, like some kind of trespasser, but then it's liberating, calming. You should all try it sometime. I sense an upcoming assignment . . .

Anyway, here is your first set of cinnamons. Write them in your notebooks as I say them: excrement . . . feces . . . waste . . . dung . . . manure. These are cinnamons for what commonly used word? Poopy, yes. Ka Ka, good Charlie. Now, the most common cinnamon of all? Good! Now again, louder. Everyone. Come on people, it's cathartic. Say it. Now everyone together: one, two, three. . . Wonderful! I can almost smell it!

When my wife left me for this guy, Richard DoRight, she filed papers for divorce claiming spousal abuse. She got three of her best friends to testify in court that I had verbally abused her, and she laid claim to half of everything I own—the equity in the house I had bought with the only inheritance I will ever receive, my pittance of a life savings.

I did get nasty on occasion. It's true. And perhaps for that, I deserved what I got. I am a pathetic problem solver. One time I saw her and the Richard coming out of La Casita. I was with our two children, had taken them to a movie on a Friday night, their mother needing a night out with friends. I saw her and DoRight and another couple coming out of the restaurant, and I put the kids in the car and walked over. I should have taken her aside before addressing her, no doubt—my bad, I confess, letting my emotions get the best of me.

I walked up to her and said, "You heartless fucking bitch." I don't know what I expected—maybe nothing, maybe I just wanted to unload—but I certainly didn't expect to see on her face the expression I saw, as she's standing there with my replacement. A look of sorrow. *Sorrow* goddammit. I mean, she's standing alongside the man that is, by virtue of simply being there with her, everything I am not, and she's the one feeling sorrow.

So tell me, did my words constitute verbal abuse? Maybe. There's two sides to every story, people. Her friends, as they made clear in court, saw it as a brutal attack. From their perspective, she was stuck in a bad marriage, trying to get relief by spending some time with a few people who accepted her for who she was, and this guy, the guy she's trying to get relief from, tracks her down and assaults her with the most hurtful words.

And my side? Well, my side is that you deserve what you get, at least the bad stuff. Even though half the time you don't know what you're doing wrong until afterward, when you get punished for it. And sometimes even then you don't know—ask Job, ask Gregor Samsa, ask Corey Johnson, or Back Row Johnny. There's good stuff too, of course there is—mindless merriment, serendipity. But you get no credit for it—the good stuff is merely good fortune. It's the age-old Christian curse, minions: thank God for the good stuff; blame yourself for the bad.

Before you go, your assignment: tomorrow, I want you all to skip school. Yes, Charlie, skip school. It's very simple: go somewhere you wouldn't normally go. Take the road less travelled by, the way my son and I did last week. And at some point, pause to appreciate how strange it is, how eerie. You'll know I'm here in class, with those few of you too cowardly to do the assignment, and you'll feel like a ghost, so programmed to be in this classroom with me that your feet will barely touch the ground. Your assignment, minions, is to feel guilty, so guilty you begin to float.

7

Good morning, Judases. Head phones off Charlie. I got a call last night from a parent of someone in this room. No need to say who as the call only helps today's lesson. The parent told me that discussing my personal life with my students is, as she put it, "reckless and irresponsible." I had to agree. Of course it is.

Last year, you read Oedipus. The guy slept with his own mother. This year, you read Hamlet, who damn near did the same, going to Gertrude's room, prying into her sex life with his uncle, into the *incestuous pleasure of his bed.* You read Yeats prophesying the goddammed apocalypse. In ninth grade you read Medea, who to spite her husband, murdered her own children. You read all kinds of shit, and your parents accept it because it's *not real.* It's like going to the zoo to see the lion kept safely in its cage. Ooooh, look at those huge incisors! Look at the woman poisoning her own children!

Well, the lion means a hell of a lot more when there's no cage holding him harmlessly at bay. And the same with jealousy and betrayal and sex and revenge. Keep it safely confined to a book and it can't hurt you. Don't get me wrong, I am, as you well know, a big believer in catharsis. But at some point, well, you've got to have the real thing.

Everything you learn is in a cage, quarantined, tied up, sterilized—choose your goddamned metaphor. *School* is a fucking cage. How the hell can you learn anything when you're being held prisoner? All you learn is how to conform, how to get by, how to *pass the fucking test*. Or, if you're a bit more creative, like Hannah here, you learn to do exactly what we teach you not to do—to avoid, undermine, subvert. You learn *despite* school, not because of it.

There's no question that Hannah's knowledge of how to screw someone in the basement bathroom is deeper, truer, more lasting than Jennifer's knowledge of the rhyme scheme of "Minnerver Cheevy." Yes, Hannah you *know* how to go in one at a time, at an interval, how to run the water in the sink, how to flush the unused toilet, how, if there happens to be a teacher nearby, to shift as you exit the bathroom into obsequious student mode and ask a distracting question—"Oh Miss Hagenmeyer, will the homework for tonight be posted online?"—as your serpentine paramour slithers out behind you.

Because Hannah *uses* her knowledge. What does Jennifer do with hers? It's only relevant if she's asked a particular question on a test, or if the same academic issue comes up in some class next year—if she even remembers it next year. There's a reason why the term "academic" is pejorative. And that's exactly what you learn in school, shit that is "academic."

So go home tonight, Jennifer, and tell your mother she is absolutely right. Telling you guys about my personal life was reckless. In fact, it was more than that. It was narcissistic.

It may have even been abusive, breaking down the time-honored boundary between teacher and student, the trust, the illusion of safety. But then, Jennifer, tell her I reconstructed the cage, that with one simple utterance, *"I made it all up,"* the boundaries were re-established. It's what a lot of you did last week in your Dream Narratives. You wrote these amazing, wild stories about shame and confusion, rage and terror, but then you ended them by putting the bars right back up, with one final murderous sentence: "And then I woke up."

Do you realize how strong the experience is if you don't wake up? If you go out through the gate and never come back?

But we have to, we have to always wake up, return to our senses, return to the compound. So Jennifer, tell your mother I woke up, we all woke up. Tell her I never stood on the 59th Street Bridge, never accosted my ex outside La Casita, never took my boy for ice cream during the school day. Tell her I told the stories as part of a lesson, as part of an act. Tell her those experiences I discussed have been safely returned to their cages, relegated to the realm of fiction, and we have nothing at all to fear. Her lovely daughter is safe.

8

This is it, people. My final day. Our esteemed principal, Dr. Clarkson, brought me before the board last night, a sheaf of evidence this fucking thick, from former students, parents, current students... Yes, we have a Judas amongst us, playing her role just like the rest of us, trying to get her lines right.

How can I blame you for playing the roles you've been assigned? How can I blame my ex for leaving me? Yes, she was an opportunist, but in the end it was my obstinance that tore us apart, my refusal to follow the script, to follow her script anyway. I think we had different scripts, people. What the hell do you do when you're given different scripts?

And so I have granted her full custody of my children. She and Richie DoRight have a nice home in the village of Sag Harbor, with it's A+ rated school system and teachers that teach, that believe in rectitude, convention, staying on track. And who knows, maybe their lessons will stick.

As for you, my minions, my former minions, I would like to wish you success as you continue on your paths. Would *like* to, but finally cannot. I just don't believe in it—in grades, aptitude tests, college. To wish this for you would be to wish you American cheese. No, I do not wish you success but failure. I wish you loneliness, ignominy, exile, *the whips and scorns of time, the pangs of despised love, the proud man's contumely.*

What I wish for you, minions, is abject degradation and unendurable humiliation—that you be stretched to tearing on the ruthless rack of indifferent fate, the decrepit, starving multitudes from across the great arc of our globe converging to peck at your exposed, unprotected flesh, leaving you destitute and bloody.

And then, *only then,* I wish you the strength and grace to carry on.

PART TWO

1

Oh my oh my oh my, who would have thunk? Ronny Fremont back at Hampton Country Day—5 years passing like 5 days—to deliver the commencement address. Well, howdy doody everyone. Howdy fucking doody.

Don't fret Dr. Clarkson, just breaking the ice, chipping away at some of that old Hampton Country Day hoarfrost, my mission today to deliver the speech as promised, *Who is it That Can Tell You Who You Are?*

What a lovely, well-dressed audience, come out to see your progeny cross one threshold and move off toward the next. More diverse than when I was last here—I see some darker complexions, and there in the rear section, in the very last row, a woman in a burka, a multi-colored one at that. Perhaps she belongs to a religion that worships the living rather than the dead. The boundaries are breaking down, people. Welcome to Hampton Country Day, Madam. And Hampton Country Day, welcome to the 21st century.

Could it be, one, no two, of my former students? Is that you Charlie? Hannah? You must be goddam college graduates by now. Unless I succeeded in talking you out of it, he he. Speaking of trying to stop the inevitable, where's Miss Iscariot, Jennifer?

Is she out there? I thought I felt a draft of cold air. No? Whew, big relief. Although she couldn't get me fired from giving a speech, could she? You sure she's not out there?

You see, proud graduates of 2019, esteemed families, distinguished faculty, sell-out administrators, some of you may not know my history here at Hampton Country Day where five years ago I was released from my duties as an English teacher. At which juncture, I did what all itinerant academics do, found another institution of higher learning, one that took me in with open arms—The Riverview Psychiatric Hospital in Augusta Maine—where I remained in residence for thirty-seven edifying months.

But that's not why Dr. Clarkson and the board invited me here today, because my elevator skipped a few floors, because a couple of my sled dogs broke loose. No, they invited me because I resurrected myself, got my shit together, and published a *New York Times* notable book, my story of redemption aligning with that most revered American myth, that no matter how deeply into the soil you've been trampled, you can rise back up and trample trample trample other people down. Horatio Ronald Fremont, proudly reporting for commencement services, Dr. Clarkson, sir!

It was four months after my termination here at Hampton Country Day when the last bulb on my marquee blinked out, I packed a bag, and headed off like Lear into the storm, driving all night through a torrential nor'easter, arriving at the Riverview entry gate unable to speak, my left side soaked from the Civic's leaky window, the guard radioing another who brought me into a wood-paneled room to sit in a chair bolted to the floor before a bench bolted to the floor on which sat three people, one in a white orderly's uniform, the other two, men my age in suits. After a few moments, I found a voice—not *my* voice, *a* voice—and told them I had crossed a line, had done irreparable harm to more people than I cared to mention, and needed to take a break from polite society.

I removed a letter from my chest pocket, soggy from the faulty window, and handed it to them. It was an email I had printed out—from guess who? The icy one herself. Straight-A, No-nonsense, Keep-the-Trains-Running-on-Time Jennifer Iscariot. I brought it with me today.

"Dear Mr. Fremont,

I'm writing from a small town somewhere in the middle of the country, in a location I'd prefer not to disclose, where I ended up after my post-graduation road trip, having decided to take a gap year. I am living in a small community called Jambalaya, made up of people from a variety of backgrounds who hold onto their pasts, their heritage—what they "refuse to let go of," Mr. Fremont, remember? We have this wonderful melding of culture and tradition here—Christians, Muslims, atheists, all living together peacefully.

I've been thinking about your class, Mr Fremont, and have come to the realization that the reason you chose me as your foil wasn't my innocence, or my ignorance, as I thought at the time, but my studiousness—the fact that I took every lesson, every word uttered by you and every other teacher, seriously. I was so literal-minded I didn't know the difference between an assignment asking me to chart a rhyme scheme and one asking me to renounce my entire way of life. Do you know what I did the day you assigned us to skip school, Mr. Fremont? Spent the entire day sitting in the nature preserve across from campus trembling. But I did it, Mr. Fremont, I did the assignment.

Yes, it was my obedience that made me your nemesis. Because I believed in the institutions you attacked, but more because I believed in you. When you mocked me, called me Judas, said renunciation was the only way we could make anything of ourselves, I believed you.

Now I'm doing your final assignment. Surrounded by people with true convictions, I am learning to let what is untrue simply fall away. I may not be lying exposed and bloody beneath the broiling desert sun, but I am getting there, Mr. Fremont. I am getting there.

Sincerely,
Jennifer Browley

I had received the email in late September, remember sitting at my kitchen table and closing my laptop, overcome with a mix of shame and pride at the impact my words, my teaching, had had. But rereading the conclusion—"I am getting there, Mr. Fremont"—I began to feel as if I'd committed a prank that had gone terribly wrong, as if I had dared someone, no *assigned* someone, to swim across the entire ocean, and was standing on the shore watching their head and stroking arms get smaller and smaller.

2

The Maine woods do remarkable things with the acutely angled sunlight of October—shaking it, stirring it, letting it dance amongst the burning leaves. From a window-side carol in the Riverview library, I spent my mornings watching autumn reach its fiery apogee and begin its decline, and writing my memoir, the story of an English teacher, who, the more he fails to satisfy the people around him, the deeper he plunges into the literature he's teaching, the final text of the year, Shakespeare's *King Lear.* I know, Charlie and Hannah, we didn't read *Lear,* I read it, re-read it, on my own. For Christ sake, my book's a memoir, you're allowed to enhance a bit. Hell, if you want to get published, enhancing's a goddammed requirement.

In the afternoons, I met with staff, who, after two months of chin scratching, tendered an initial diagnosis of Acute Clinical Depression, changing it two weeks later to Dissociative Disorder, this time with the qualification that I was co-morbid, their rigid taxonomy of maladies apparently unable to account for my many contradictory symptoms.

One day, the head psychiatrist, Dr. Wombley, called me to his office saying he'd received a report of a conversation I'd had at lunch in which I had exhibited anti-social tendencies, announcing that I liked junk food more than my children.

The conversation had gone like this:

> Jerry (39 year-old bachelor chemist from Brookline who had recently emerged from a

three-month-long catatonic state): The mac and cheese is creamy today.

Moi: It is truly delightful.

Holly (52 year-old mother of four from Albany who played the state lottery every day for sixteen years, her winnings totaling 814 dollars, her expenditures, one hundred twenty-five thousand): All they did was add more powdered milk.

Moi: I prefer powdered milk, imitation products in general. Living things are complicated and prone to rot.

Jerry (reciting the lessons he'd been learning in Group): But it's only with the living that we can interact, seek forgiveness, offer it ourselves, and have loving relationships.

Moi: Craving trumps love every time. I mean, sure, I love my children, but I wouldn't break into the snack pantry at 2 AM to see one of them.

Each night I'd been sneaking down the darkened corridor, popping the dead bolt which I had sabotaged with a wad of masking tape, an act caught on video surveillance, which they said demonstrated my contempt for regulations, whereas

I insisted just the opposite, that my nightly burglaries demonstrated a deep and abiding patriotism. Surely you concur, my fashionably-outfitted listeners. If we have a national characteristic, it is not industry, not ambition, and sure as hell not compassion. It is craving. The unquenchable urge to get.

Doctor Wombley leaned forward. "What gives with you, Fremont?" he said.

"I need to write my book," I said. "Need to stop reading the damned things and write one."

"To feel validated?" he said.

"To see what the thinking makes," I answered, Dr. Wombley missing the allusion, but not you Charlie, not you Hannah. *Thinking makes it so*, remember?

"Well," said Dr. Wombly, "we do encourage our patients to find creative outlets. In the meantime, I'm going to change your diagnosis. What you are Fremont, is betwixt and between. One day you throw with your left hand, the next day, throw with your right. As of today, Fremont, your official diagnosis is *Inauthenticity*."

Hmm, I stretched my arms, rolled my shoulders, as if I were trying on a custom-tailored blazer. "I'll take it," I said.

And so, autumn into winter into spring, I wrote my book, not about finding myself but losing myself, about how when my children moved into Mr. DoRight's three-story traditional on Main Street in Sag Harbor, I withdrew to ancient, pre-Christian Britain to cavort with the likes of Edgar, Kent, and Lear, where together we ping-ponged through the inscrutable wilderness, as the blinded Gloucester says, mere flies to wanton boys.

The book was published the following autumn, and I spent the next fourteen months, Riverview serving as home base—what better place than a funhouse for an imposter to call home?—doing book tours, delivering lectures.

And alas, here I am, making my triumphant return to Hampton Country Day, a literary star. Thank you, thank you very much. For all queries and requests—speaking engagements, film options, product endorsements, or any other obsequious attempts to rub your lowly elbows against my *notable* ones—please contact my agent.

What a fitting ending to the presentation that would be. Unfortunately, today I'm not making a presentation, I'm telling a story. So sit back and try to get comfortable—nobody's going anywhere.

3

My time in Riverview wasn't spent merely reassembling scattered fragments, constructing a coherent narrative out of an utterly incoherent life. No, I had another itch that needed scratching—two, really. Regarding my children, I came to realize that down beneath my magnanimity—beneath the graciousness with which I had not merely accepted the judge's decision to award my ex-wife custody but had insisted to my children that the change represented opportunity, rebirth—lay a disquiet, a simmering acrimony. Yes, I realized they were children, hadn't asked to be brought into the world, yet after all my doting, it was they who had ended up with a family, not me—how could I not feel short-changed? Yes, I was the parent, supposed to rise above, not only know better but do better. But I was also a goddammed human being, wasn't I?

Wasn't I?

Perhaps you too, beneath the congenial faces, harbor a similar unease, a nagging counterweight, a foreboding—as you send your children off into the new breaking day, the darkness closing in on you from behind…

How about you sir, there in the third row, blithely enjoying today's ceremony? Any doubt buried within, any rancor? Or you Madam, in the last row of the rear section, your face hidden within your burka? Or you Miss? Yes, you with the misty visage, sitting there overcome, swollen with emotion on this momentous day, your grief-tinged pride nearly too much to contain. Or maybe you just have to pee. Go on then, 2nd door on the left in the lobby.

The other itch was Jennifer, and so I emailed her back. Kept it brief, polite, told her I understood the points she had made, admired her temerity, and wished her well.

Her reply came that same morning, and when I saw it filled the entire screen, I tucked my laptop under my arm and skulked off to the darkest, rearmost corner of the library.

"We've lost five members in the last two weeks," she said, 'two to the left, three to the right. Jambalaya is teetering."

"If it seems too good to be true . . . " I muttered *sotto voce.*

As if anticipating my pedantic response, the email continued. "As repugnant as the right wing is with their inbred bigotry and xenophobia, the left isn't much better, Mr. Fremont. I'm not even talking the far left, I'm talking the near left, the *reasonable* left, always insisting they, *you*, know better, declaring others *should* know better, everything should *be* better—the Opioid epidemic, the mass shootings, the crowds of people chanting hatred—as if outrage, as if *rage,* vindictiveness, or for that matter, stupidity, boorishness, are aberrations that can be fixed, can be scheduled away with swimming lessons and community service and a subscription to *The New Yorker.*

"You're great when it comes to social programs," she continued, "but as soon as you're confronted with issues of emotion or intellect, with *biology*—distemper, short attention spans, literal-mindedness, Mr. Fremont—you pack up your toys and go home.

"In the end," she said, "no matter how reasonable, how informed, yours is just another dogma used to create a hierarchy and exclude—the dogma of equanimity. The dogma of knowing better."

Touché, Jennifer, Tou-fucking-ché. All that humility I tried to sell her and her classmates, that vulnerability I displayed with my woe-is-me confessions—standing on the 59th Street Bridge, getting dumped by my wife—no matter how real, how *authentic,* I tried to make it, was in the end nothing more than a demonstration of how much I had learned, had overcome, a pronouncement of all I had mastered. The supreme chutzpah of the storyteller who, no matter how woeful the tale he tells, climbs up on his pedestal to tell it.

Jennifer wasn't done. "Therefore," she continued, "we at Jambalaya can no longer passively advocate for moderation as the extremes grow more rabid on either side, and the institutional overlords gaze down on it all through their tinted, shatterproof windows.

"Which leaves us with only one option," she said in closing. "We, the lowly middle, must enter the fight."

4

It was around this time, my daughter had her 13th birthday, and her mother took the two children, Cecilia and her younger brother by two years, Jacob, on the ferry to New London, where she put them on a train to meet me for a weekend in Boston.

I booked a suite at the Doubletree Downtown and the three of us spent the weekend hopping on and off the sightseeing trolley, walking the Freedom Trail. The problem was, I wanted to make up for lost time, whereas they, partly due to my own directive to never look back, never regret, felt no such compulsion.

As we toured Boston Common, the Old North Church, Paul Revere's colonial home, they began to grow weary, and so I doubled down, their lassitude, I thought, a cry for fatherly correction. As they dragged their feet, my urging turned to scolding, until finally, in the Old State House, unable to go any further, they wilted onto nearby benches, and I played the shame card.

"Because you live on Main Street in Sag Harbor with your mac-pros and Iphones," I said, "you think this history doesn't apply to you."

In response, my son began selecting green M&Ms from his bag—for some reason he'd never liked the green ones—and pelting people in the tour group across the room, my daughter beside him groaning with disgust, not at his behavior but at my inept parenting.

"Why the green ones?" I chided, resuming an argument we'd had some years earlier, in which I'd insisted all the colors tasted the same, my son, with my daughter joining him, insisting they did not.

"Because they taste like shit," he answered.

"Hmm," I said, "I thought that was the flavor of the brown ones."

"Brown ones taste like cow shit," he said. "Green ones, dog shit."

Now, he began tossing brown ones, several people in the group turning back to locate the sniper.

"And the yellow?" I asked.

"Yellow ones are piss-flavored," he said, now adding yellow to the barrage, the group leader calling over, "Excuse me!" not to him, but to me, the apparent responsible party. "I'm trying to conduct a tour!"

At this point, my daughter chimed in, calling across the room, "We're sorting out our M&Ms."

"Must you throw them?" the guide asked.

The three of us looked at each other. "We can't eat them," Cecilia called over. "They taste like shit."

"And piss!" added Jacob.

Fortunately for the tour, the bag was now empty. I shrugged at the guide and she turned back to her group.

"I remember you telling me in fourth grade," Cecila said to me, once we'd given up for the day and boarded the trolley back to Fanuel Hall, "that learning about a bunch of dead white guys from the old days wasn't history but was desultory—you taught me the word."

It was true, I had reviewed the Xeroxed history lesson Cecilia'd brought home and, in a rare moment of candor, said I found it dated and dull. A rare moment because my parental impulse, in stark contrast to my diatribes as a teacher—oh, I am nothing if not a hypocrite—was to protect, encourage them to conform, seek safety within the confines of the group. What

I wanted was for my children to be athletes and cheerleaders, bumper sticker-worthy members of the honor roll, to live lives free from the crushing burden of self-recrimination. But it doesn't work that way, does it? The things our children remember are never the lessons we repeat ad nauseum but the truth that leaks out a single time.

And so, returning to the hotel, Cecilia and Jacob, relieved of the obligation placed upon them by their over-compensating father, piled high the copious pillows on their King-sized bed, plugged in their devices for fresh supplies of power, and dove deep into their feathery virtual worlds. And me, I went down to the bar.

5

It wasn't until this past fall that I heard again from Jennifer. The day after a shooting many of you no doubt recall, in West Allis, Wisconsin—8 dead, 13 injured. The shooter stationed himself atop an overpass with a semi-automatic rifle and hundreds of rounds, draping a banner over the railing that read, "THE LOWLY MIDDLE" and targeting a line of cars waiting to enter the state fair grounds for a white nationalism rally. Until finally, the police came and he turned the rifle back into his mouth.

Jennifer's email was chatty, unfocused. She said she'd read a review of my book, offered her congratulations, told me about the fusion cooking group she had started at Jambalaya, the different cultures mixing and matching foods and spices, exchanging traditions, even idols and garments, infusing them with new meaning.

"What do you know about the Wisconsin fairgrounds?" I immediately replied.

"Every few months, we draw numbers," came her response. "High number has the choice to pick their own target or be given one. This time it was white nationalists. Next time, it will be a gathering on the left. I am one of two that have yet to draw high number."

Then, before I could react, she did something almost endearing—alluded to a work we'd read in class. "Do you remember, Mr. Fremont, what the Misfit says after he shoots the grandmother in that Flannery O'Connor story? 'She'd have been a good woman if there'd been someone to shoot her every minute of her life.'"

Of course I remembered, though the line wasn't "if *there* had been," but "if *it* had been someone to shoot her."

"The point," she continued, "is that sometimes the only way to pop the bubble of self-righteousness, of sanctimony, of always knowing better, Mr. Fremont, is with death, the prospect of imminent, unavoidable death."

I shut my laptop, drew in a long breath.

You see, my well-coiffed parishioners, to read in a work of fiction, in "A Good Man is Hard to Find," or *Hamlet,* or *Beloved,* or even to fully descend into the illusory world of Lear where death, the ultimate act of reprisal, looms over every scene—that is one thing. But this was neither a work of fiction nor a delusion. On the contrary, the words had come from the most sober, most rational, most *literal* student I had ever had.

All I could do was sit there in the darkened corner of the Riverview library, unsure if I'd been confided in, included in a dark secret, or threatened. How strange, disorienting, the prospect of death, the notion that your life, painstakingly memorialized, constructed and reconstructed, may not be your own. And so I sat in that dusky space, betwixt and between as Dr. Wombley had said, humming that silly 60s Donovan song.

Jennifer, Juniper . . .
Is she sleeping, I don't think so
Is she breathing, yes very low
Whatcha doing, Jennifer my love?

6

If you don't mind, I'd like you all to turn your attention to the back row of the rear section, to the woman in the multi-colored burka. I can't help but wonder, Madam, which of our graduates you are here to support. Or perhaps you are not here for them at all. Would you kindly stand up, Madam?

And, if you wouldn't mind, please uncover your face.

So it's true, I did feel a draft of cold air. No, no, Dr. Clarkson, please. This is the climactic moment of the story. We have to let it play out.

Tell me, Jennifer, is it a personal slight that has motivated your visit today? Is it vindictiveness? No, I am not looking down my nose on the glandular desire for revenge, as if I know better—if I've learned anything from you these past five years, Jennifer, it's to know better than to know better.

People, please, if this is her intention, let her proceed. My, but you do approach with purpose, Jennifer, the steely gait, your face exposed but not your hands, the gown on one side bulging just a bit—Dr. Clarkson, please, *this is part of the story.* She's not seeking revenge at all but justice—for the voiceless middle. Isn't that right, Jennifer, you're acting on principle, not passion.

Either way, you've turned back from the uncrossable sea toward land, Jennifer, returned like a homing pigeon to the scene of your mistreatment, the source of your shame, sat quietly in the rear awaiting your cue, and now stride with single-minded intention from the back row all the way ... to the front.

Watcha doing, Jennifer?

7

For those whose view was blocked, or averted their eyes, please Jennifer, show them the object you withdrew from beneath your gown. *Memoir of an Inauthentic Man*.

And what's this, a highlighted passage? Ah yes, the words I muttered upon my arrival at Riverview, the same ones old Lear uttered. Indeed, the inspiration for today's speech: *Who is it that can tell me who I am?*

So that was why you came up here, Jennifer, to keep us on topic. Scaring the holy shit out of us, not to derail the proceedings, simply to make sure we stay on track.

Or was the highlighted passage a question for yourself? Perhaps you came today, Jennifer, Jennifer *Browley*, to get yourself back on track.

Either way, we had ourselves a moment—speechlessness, silence, helplessness... No, the moment didn't last—of course it didn't—truth never does. I am once again blabbering away. Blabbering, sputtering, spewing—impulsively, reflexively, trying to spread my seed however I can, a creature, as you've argued so convincingly, Jennifer, whose pompous motivations originate in the glands, not the mind.

But not you, Jennifer. You stand still, listening and waiting. You watch. A tad prudish, anal retentive, no doubt—I mean, sometimes a tangent can be a bit of fun, you know—but in the end, you are studious to your core. What did you learn today, Jennifer?

And tell me, why the trembling?

You need to sit down. Come, come. It's okay, I've got you . . . a few more steps . . .

Sit. It's okay, just sit.

Wasn't just a book, was it? No, no Dr. Clarkson, it was a purse I felt beneath the gown. You're carrying a purse in there, right Jennifer?

Breathe, Jennifer. You were simply doing the assignment given you by Jambalaya. *Trying* to do the assignment. What has you shaking is not the awfulness of what you were assigned, but the fact you couldn't do it. You, Jennifer Browley, finally met an assignment you could not do, and now sit there bereft, nobody to tell you what comes next, all alone on the barren surface of the world.

8

Tonight, I will meet my children, will step from the tidy tweed of the keynote speaker, the omniscience of the pedagogue, into the role of the feckless parent, seeking only a moment of peace with the people I love. I will pick them up at la casa de DoRight and take them into the village for ice cream, will allow them any size cone they desire, will let them wear their ear buds, or AirPods, in the car, in the ice cream shop, let them sit on the bench out front and pelt the passersby with an assortment of shit and piss-flavored M&Ms.

And then I will drop them at their home, where they will retreat to their rooms, withdrawing into the gauzy glow of their electronic cocoons.

They didn't ask to be born into this anxious mess, and I will appease them however I can. Even if it means giving them up entirely.

Now, graduates, it is time to receive your diplomas. This is the last lecture you will ever sit through as children. By the powers vested in me as author of a *New York Times* notable book, as exemplar of that most revered, most hollow, rags to riches American myth, I hereby cut you free, release you to sally forth, without regret or compunction, without shame or guilt. Take your diplomas and go.

Don't look back. Just go.

Two Mile Hollow

Pulling up to Indian Wells for the afternoon haul, Ben saw Donny's truck in the sand by the water, but instead of joining him, sat there in the parking lot watching the incoming waves. Small but resolute, they churned toward shore, one after another, their crests peeling back in the wind like the teeth of spinning saw blades.

Ben's father had been the head of the haul-seining crew until he'd died three years ago and Ben's older brother by four years, Donny, had come home from Nova Scotia where he'd gone in search of better fishing after high school. Their mother lived nearby with a guy who'd quit haul seining and opened up a deli that had expanded each of the past three years, and now included a small restaurant and catering service.

Ben watched the figures of his brother and their helper get out of the truck and slide the dory from the trailer into the mild surf, figured they could manage fine without the gas he'd picked up, and headed back to Lazy Point.

That night at the deli his mother, after marrying the owner, now half-owned, Ben saw his girlfriend, or ex-girlfriend, he wasn't sure, Cindy, sitting with Donny's girl. The day before they'd gone to the Episcopal church's annual Chowder Festival and Ben, appalled at Cindy's flirtatious behavior, had driven her home in silence. Now, when she joined him in a booth, they ordered their usual plate of French fries, which grew cold as they picked at it. As if to make some kind of point, Cindy told him his mother had offered her a job at the deli.

"Go ahead, take it," Ben said, "but it's a bullshit job. Serving tourists, people who don't give a damn."

"I suppose I should haul seine," Cindy said. "How many of you are there left, three? Now there's a smart career choice."

Though he knew fishing was a dead-end, Ben felt a loyalty to his father, and to something else too, something vague and unsettled in the pit of his stomach.

His most vivid memory of his father was of a day when Ben had missed the afternoon haul and come home to find the old man unloading the nets by himself. Although Ben had just turned sixteen and quit high school to fish full-time, he'd also just met Cindy and on this day had skipped the afternoon haul so the two of them could take advantage of her empty house.

Driving up the street at dusk, Ben had seen the old man unloading the truck, and felt himself driving into a scene that suddenly seemed quaint, passé. He stopped on his way in to grab an armful of net.

"I can handle it," his father said, not looking at him. But Ben continued until the old man yanked the net from his hands and dumped it back in the truck. Excited by the quick movement, their black Labrador, Guts, danced over and began barking.

"Jesus Christ," Ben mumbled, "you ain't got to kill yourself just to prove a point."

His father pointed a thick finger at Ben's chin. "Then don't come strolling in here at sundown and lay your clean hands on my nets." His raised voice sent Guts into another spasm of tail-wagging and barking.

"Maybe I got something better to do," Ben said, and as he turned to the house, Guts jumped at him playfully, Ben fending him off with a forearm, the dog returning to earth and springing in the same motion toward Ben's father. Leaning into the truck for more net, the old man felt the dog's paws on his hip and wheeled around in a fury, meeting the dog's jaw with his fist and knocking it unconscious to the ground.

Waiting for his hamburger, Ben caught Cindy's eye and, feeling a surge of forgiveness, nodded and said, "What's up, girl?" But the words came out flat, uncaring.

"Nothing," Cindy said. She stood up and returned to Donny's girlfriend's booth.

Donny strolled into the deli, still wearing his knee-high rubber boots. He took a look around the restaurant, spotted the girls, and squeezed in opposite Ben.

"Where were you?" Donny said.

"Nowhere," Ben said. "Anything running?"

"You talk to Cindy?" Donny said.

"Nah," Ben said. "Any bass?"

"Where the hell were you?" Donny asked again.

"Nowhere," Ben said.

Donny huffed and took another look over at the two women. "Guess I better check in," he said. Donny stood up and, dragging the heavy boots, walked over to Cindy and Joy, exchanged a few words, and walked back.

"Told her you and me need to get a beer," Donny said.

The two brothers bought a six-pack from the retail side of the store and took Ben's truck out to the beach, Donny pushing in the CD already in the player.

The nearest beach was Two Mile Hollow, also known as Queer's Beach, usually deserted in the off-season. The two sat idling in the empty parking lot, sipping their beers and peering ahead to where the truck's lights shone into the blackness. Side one finished and side two began.

"What part of Canada was it again, the place you lived?" Ben said.

"Nova Scotia," Donny said.

"Some kind of farm," Ben said.

"There were eight of us and a couple acres of crops," Donny said. "But it was near enough to the ocean so's I could still fish."

"And you were screwing some married chick."

"Two of 'em," Donny said with a sigh, lowering himself into the seat. "One from Maine, the other from Ohio. Hell, they're the only two I've been with besides Joy."

"Damn," Ben said.

"Then one of em's husband inherited a bunch of money and they all moved back. I stayed up there fishing till Mom called and said Dad died."

After the last song on side two, side one began again, Donny slipping into a slumber, Ben still sitting upright, staring into the night.

"Canada," Ben said, glancing at Donny's unhearing form and shaking his head. "How do you just move to Canada?"

Two days after punching the dog, the old man had for the first time in Ben's memory stayed home in bed. When Ben and Guts—after being knocked out the dog had been skittish with anyone other than Ben—came home after the afternoon haul, Ben had found his mother moving about the kitchen oddly jittery, too preoccupied to greet him or ask about the fishing. Ben walked down the hall to his father's room and looked in, finding it empty, bed made.

"Where's Pop?" he asked, returning to the kitchen. But his mother didn't answer, just nervously ushered Ben to the single setting at the table and served him dinner.

Afterward, Ben took Guts for a drive, but unable to shake the image of his parents' empty, tidy bedroom, turned back and confronted his mother, who, without lifting her head from the sinkful of dishes, told him his father had died that morning of a heart attack. She hadn't told him when he came in, she explained, because she didn't want him to hear the news on an empty stomach, and by the end of the month, still jittery, peripatetic, she'd moved in with the guy that until a year earlier ran the only other remaining haul-seining crew besides his father's, and who now owned the deli.

"Ben," Donny said sleepily, rolling his head on the seat-back toward his brother, "if you're on the crew, you got to be there both hauls, morning and afternoon. Dory ran out of gas today—we had to row in."

But behind Donny, a surge of light from an approaching car caught Ben's attention.

"It's November," Ben said, "Goddam season's over."

"Not no more it ain't," Donny said, rolling his head back the other way to see. "Nowadays they're out here till Christmas."

"But what the hell for?" Ben said. He peered past Donny to where the car, dark colored with dark windows, had pulled up a couple of spaces over.

Ben got out of the truck and passed through the headlights on his way to the car. Donny watched as he rapped a knuckle against the window, which descended an inch or so, and a minute later Ben returned to the truck.

"I asked him what he was looking for," Ben said, "and he just goes, 'Nothing, I couldn't sleep.'" Ben stared at Donny for an explanation, shook his head, and opened another beer. "Get me out of here," he said.

They drove back through the village, found the deli closed, and continued on past the horse farms, which opened out beneath the night, then on to Springs, turning at a fork toward Cindy's.

"Just to see if she's home," Ben said, chugging the rest of his beer and flipping the can behind his seat where it rattled against the others. They pulled over before a split-level ranch, the windows dark but the house faintly lit by a streetlight.

"Probably at Joy's," Donny said.

"Nah," Ben said, "she went to bed."

Donny had always been struck by Ben's prescience. While he himself focused on the business at hand, figuring things out as he went, Ben seemed to know things in advance, things for which, as far as Donny could tell, there hadn't been any indication.

Ben walked up the driveway, the streetlamp casting a dark shadow at his side, stepped onto the porch and thumped the door with the heel of his hand.

After a full minute of silence, a light went on inside and the door opened, Cindy stepping onto the porch wrapped in an oversized parka, legs bare.

"We were just driving by," Ben said. "Thought maybe you'd come have a beer."

"I already went to bed," Cindy said. She shook her head in frustration and stepped back up onto the door sill, where she peered back at Ben. "What is it with you?" she said.

"Ain't nothin' with me," Ben said. He shrugged and glanced back at the truck. Cindy swung the door closed.

"Gotta get her beauty sleep, huh?" Donny said as Ben accelerated down the lane.

"Shit," Ben said, "I ain't hardly slept all week."

"And you're some beautiful, too," Donny said.

"Compared to the rest of the Brister men, I'm a freakin' cherub."

"A what?"

"Like they got on the windows at St. Anne's."

"What do you know about St. Anne's?"

"Plenty," Ben said.

A few days after his father's funeral, Donny still in Canada, Ben had gone back to the Episcopal church and found the priest, a young guy with hair long enough to tuck behind his ears, watching a football game in the rectory out back. The priest remembered Ben from the service, introduced himself as Jack, and invited Ben in. He flipped off the television and offered Ben a beer, which Ben declined.

"So what's up?" Jack asked, settling himself into a sofa.

"I want to know if my father dying means there's some kind of score that needs to be settled."

"Score?" Jack asked.

"Like do I need to make amends?"

"I don't know," Jack said, "you got any unfinished business with him?"

"I'm just asking," Ben said, "what's the normal procedure."

"If you're feeling some guilt," the priest said, "it'd be normal to ask for forgiveness."

"Why would I feel guilt?" Ben said.

"When you lose someone," Jack said, "it's common to wish you'd done some things differently."

"What are you trying to say?" Ben said.

At this point the priest stood up, walked into the next room, and returned with two beers, handing one to Ben. "Take it," he said, "you're not on trial here."

As Ben sipped his beer, Jack told him in surprisingly blunt language about his own father back in Oregon, how the hostility between them had steadily grown until one night Jack found himself pacing outside his father's bedroom with clenched fists.

Jack took a long pull on his beer.

"Here I was," he said, "ready to challenge him to a fight, when all of a sudden it came to me: This isn't about him—it's about me. A week later I entered the seminary."

"So you're saying I should start going to church," Ben said.

"I'm saying it's how you look at it. It might seem real dark where you're looking but off to the side there's a faint light flickering somewhere. You just have to look."

Ben sat there trying to make sense of the metaphor, searching the past week for a flickering light. But no matter what he recalled—the long morning drives during which he'd tried to summon grief for his departed father, the idle afternoons spent lying with Cindy gazing out her bedroom window—all he found was a dull half light, the landscape shadowless beneath an ashen sky.

Ben and Donny stopped for another six-pack and returned to Two Mile Hollow, this time shutting the lights. They weren't there ten minutes when the same car pulled up beside them, shining its lights out over the ocean.

"The insomniac," Ben said.

"Looking for love," Donny mumbled.

"He ain't finding it in my asshole," Ben said.

"Not real love," Donny said.

"Fuck you."

"You know, if you think about it," Donny said, "these guys might be on to something. I mean, imagine chasing girls just as horny as you. They'd chase you right back."

"You don't get nothing for free," Ben said.

"Maybe *you* don't," Donny said, and his voice softened as he thought back to Canada, "but there's times when everything just falls into place and you get your pick of pleasures."

"You can run off somewhere and think you do," Ben said, "but there's always a price."

"That St. Anne's talking?" Donny said.

"It's me talking," Ben said. "St. Anne's ain't nothing but a bunch of shit about flickering lights."

"Let me tell you, I'd a married that chick from Ohio. The other one wasn't bad, but the Ohio chick used to come to my room and fucking dance for me." Donny shook his head, gazing out before him. "I'd lie there watching till I couldn't take it anymore and she'd just pull her clothes off and climb in bed."

"She was married already," Ben said.

"I'm saying if she was *single* I'd a married her."

"Right, and then she'd a been dancing in somebody else's room."

"You don't know that," Donny said.

"I'm just saying what difference does it make. Now that it's gone, what difference does it make what it was?"

"A lot of difference," Donny said. "Cause I know it's out there."

"That ain't what's out there."

Donny released a long stream of air and Ben, looking back to the car at their side, its headlights pushing vainly against the darkness, popped out the CD and opened his door.

"Come on," he said, "this guy's starting to get on my nerves."

Donny watched Ben climb out, then followed, not trusting him on his own. As they reached the driver's window, it lowered to about half open, and they saw a smooth round face that looked oddly young beneath a receding hairline.

"Guess you ain't got to sleep yet," Ben said.

"No," the man said. "I'm not used to the quiet."

"You from the city?" Ben said.

"Guilty as charged," the man said. "You guys must live out here."

"Born and raised," Ben said.

"You're lucky to live in such a beautiful place," the man said.

Ben and Donny stood a moment in silence, Ben straightening and peering off at the ocean, then leaning back to the window.

"Listen," Ben said, "me and my brother here are headed down to the water if you care to join us."

Without a moment's hesitation, the window went up, lights and motor shut off, and Ben raised his eyebrows at Donny as the man slid out of the car. He was short and wore a turtleneck and fleece vest.

"I've just been driving around," he said, clapping his hands against the chill.

Ben led them into the soft sand and down toward the water, Donny in his boots taking up the rear. Moving out from the dim light of the parking lot, Ben walked nearly to the water and turned back to the stranger.

"I got a question for you," Ben said.

The man came to a stop.

"Give me one reason I shouldn't beat the shit out of you right now," Ben said.

The man was quiet a moment before answering. "Because I didn't do anything to you," he said.

Ben stepped forward and grabbed the man's vest in both hands. He pulled him close, their noses nearly touching, then jerked him sideways and down to the ground where he landed on his knees and stayed put.

"Come on," Donny said, grabbing Ben's arm, "this ain't gonna solve nothing."

"Just by being here," Ben said to the man, "you're doing something to me."

"Let's go," Donny said, pulling Ben away.

"You hear me?" Ben said. "Just by being here." And he yielded to Donny's hand on his arm, and the two of them walked back to the truck.

They climbed in the cab and Donny reached over and switched the ignition to accessory, playing the CD at low volume, the faint guitar chords seeming to drift in from somewhere out in the night.

They heard the door to the car open and saw the man slide in behind the wheel, start the car, and drive off.

"This is the place everybody wants to be," Donny mused. "I'll bet you even that chick from Ohio comes here at some point."

"To find you?" Ben said.

"Maybe," Donny said. "Or maybe just to come here."

"But what the fuck for?" Ben asked.

"Cause it's beautiful, and not crowded."

"Everybody can't come to a place and it not be crowded."

"They're not all here yet," Donny said.

"And once they are, then what?" Ben said.

"They start going to another place," Donny said.

"That's not what they do," Ben said.

Before driving Cindy home from the Chowder Festival the day before, Ben had felt a hand on his shoulder and turned to see the priest, Jack. He'd been standing on the line for the clam chowder made by a new bistro in the village, Ben buying it because he was hungry, not curious, and because Cindy didn't want to leave.

The feel of Jack's hand had felt immodest, as if they'd never had their disagreement in the rectory. It occurred to Ben that Jack might be gay, a person who simply skipped over the normal obstacles.

"Everybody doing okay?" Jack had asked, looking into Ben's eyes as if he actually wanted to know, despite having lived in the town for less than a year.

"Everybody's fine," Ben said, stepping back enough for Jack to withdraw his hand. "Now we're just one less," Ben said.

"Grief follows its own schedule," Jack said.

Ben ordered his chowder and before he could pay, Jack told the server he would take one too, and that Ben's chowder was on the church.

"This isn't even for me," Ben said, "it's for my girlfriend," which of course was untrue, Ben the hungry one, yet perhaps true in the sense that it was because of her, *for* her, that he was at the fair in the first place.

"Tell her I hope she likes it," Jack said, and again Ben was disturbed by the presumption, the way Jack had gone along with the lie, with the strain of what he'd said that was not true, never sensing the strain that was.

Then Ben had returned to Cindy and mentioned to her that the priest had bought the chowder, expecting her to confirm the banality of the gesture. Instead, she made Ben take her over to be introduced, whereupon she had made small talk and offered a flirtatious smile that made Ben realize the priest wasn't gay at all, simply charming.

He had driven Cindy back to her house in silence, Cindy asking once what was wrong but Ben unable to look at her, unable to speak.

Ben drove Donny from Two Mile Hollow back to his pickup truck at the deli, assured him he'd be there for the morning haul, then instead of heading out to the house on Lazy Point, turned back to East Hampton and made a final circuit through the empty town.

He drove past the pond, then the church, light from the rectory in back silhouetting its steeple against the night sky. Entering the village, dimly lit by the streetlamps, Ben gazed at the row of boutiques on either side, the rooflines of the connected buildings the same as when he had been a kid.

Everything had changed, but you could never tell by looking. You had to know.

Frankie's World

When Karla's husband and daughter headed off to their annual summer rental in Montauk, Karla stayed in the city to teach a four-week course on Thomas Hardy and complete a paper on the virgin and the whore. Tenure review was in the fall and she needed a quality publication. The last few months she'd been reading about the history of men coercing women into either an artificial innocence or an artificial depravity, but what she hadn't discovered was what these roles held that women continually found so appealing.

"Nothing's wrong," she assured Rob the night before he and Sophie drove out to the ocean. "Once I get this paper published everything'll be back to normal."

She kissed Rob on the forehead, rolled over, and went to sleep.

The next afternoon as Karla lay on the sofa in the study she shared with Rob, distractedly reading and rereading the same paragraph, her sister Frankie called. Karla and Frankie maintained a sporadic phone relationship, Frankie usually calling on weekends from her east side studio to fill Karla in on her latest fling.

"It's over with Danny," Frankie said.

"I never knew it started with Danny," Karla said.

"We went for lunch at Martell's, right?" Frankie said. "And it was incredible—*sorbet* between courses. Then we're walking along Second Avenue looking for a cab and instead of just enjoying the moment, he starts telling me about his ex-wife, about their settlement, whose getting the fucking furniture."

"Frankie, he just took you to this wonderful lunch."

"No," Frankie snapped. "Just because he spends money, that doesn't make me some receptacle for his problems."

Karla took a deep breath and raised herself from the sofa, walking over to the window and gazing at the brownstones across the street. They'd inherited theirs from Rob's mother, who'd died the same year they were married. Just this past spring Karla'd begun to feel for the first time as if the house were actually hers.

"So what do I say," Karla said, "way to go, Frankie?"

"Each time you meet a new guy," Frankie mused, ignoring the question, "you're convinced he's the one that's going to be different. Then he starts revealing himself and it's like, *get me the plastic gloves.*"

Frankie talked Karla into going for dinner and Karla taxied through the dusky park, which with its thick canopy of trees seemed to get dark earlier, and they met at Stan's on the east side. They had a drink before dinner, a bottle of wine with, and afterwards moved back to the bar, where they sat overlooking the dining room. The bar gradually filled with people moving over after dinner and others coming in off the street, the din swelling up into the high vaulted ceiling.

"Sometimes I imagine myself just taking off," Karla said, "leaving the city behind."

"Then you should," Frankie said. "If you dream it you're supposed to do it."

"That's a bit extreme, Frankie."

"*Life* is a bit extreme," Frankie said.

"It's not like I'm miserable," Karla said. "Sometimes I just can't help but wonder."

"Look at you," Frankie said, and she spun on her stool toward Karla. "You've got this great profession, a doting husband, Sophie, a west side brownstone. All you have left to do is die."

Frankie took a swallow from her drink and turned to peer at a group of dart players, or more particularly, Karla noticed, at one of them, a tall guy with a loose bowl-cut head of hair. "It's great to be successful," Frankie continued, talking back over her shoulder. "Believe me, I admire you. But you have to keep moving."

"I'm working on this paper," Karla said. "And if it gets published somewhere good . . ."

"*You* have to get going," Frankie said, glancing back with raised eyebrows. "You hear me? Not some fucking paper." Then she slid off her stool and waded into the crowd, making her way to the dartboard.

The next night, Karla sat before her laptop pondering different drafts of her paper, clicking from version to version, when the phone rang.

"In the end, it comes down to one thing," Frankie said. "Biology."

"Don't tell me you picked up that dart player," Karla said.

"Everybody's always looking for this transformation, this *completion*," Frankie said. "But when you just accept it for what it is . . ."

"Frankie, what happened?"

"We fucked in the bathroom at Stan's."

"Frankie."

"And when we came out there were about ten people standing in line, and they've all got these deeply offended looks on their faces."

"They probably had to pee," Karla said.

"Well," said Frankie, "we had to fuck."

On Friday, Karla came home after a marathon conference with a bright but rambling student, the conference starting off with an exciting synergy, but gradually, through one, then another cup of coffee, entering what Karla called the Ben-and-Jerry's-syndrome, the first half of the pint sumptuous, but the second half, once you're full yet still driven by the initial thrill, degenerating into gluttony.

Karla sat for a barren hour before the computer at the table, then mixed a margarita and brought it into the bathroom where she drew a bath, adding the Avocado oil from the box of soaps and lotions Sophie had given her for Christmas. She wondered how they were doing at the rental, if perhaps they weren't having more fun without her. She imagined them sunning and swimming, carefree, and when she envisioned herself throwing open the cottage door, surprising them, both Rob and Sophie looked up from a board game with uncomprehending faces. Releasing a long sigh, Karla undressed, letting her clothes fall to the floor, and eased her body into the warm water.

An hour later Karla awoke in a bubbleless tub of tepid water. She lay for a moment looking down at her numb pink body as if its lifelessness were too great to overcome, the synapses having widened so far that the impulse to move could no longer make the leap.

Frankie called Saturday afternoon and that night Karla arrived at Stan's first, the way Frankie preferred it. Karla took a seat at the bar beside a pleasant looking man in jeans and a crisp checkered shirt, and when Frankie entered the restaurant, Karla watched her first locate Karla at the bar, then, secure in the knowledge she wasn't alone, survey the rest of the room.

As Frankie sat beside her, Karla made a point of speaking first, the odd feeling yesterday in the tub still nagging at her. Gazing into the mirror at their reflections, Karla said, "I'm glad you're getting me out. I've been feeling so, I don't know, lackluster. I can't even tell if I miss Rob and Sophie."

Also looking into the mirror, Frankie said, "You don't but think you should." Frankie's eyes shifted from the mirror to Karla, who turned to meet them. "You always have to do the right thing," Frankie said. "Since you were eight years old you've been this impeccable model of a human being."

At first offended, as she often was by Frankie's bluntness, Karla gazed back into Frankie's unblinking eyes and thought maybe she was right. Maybe Karla was simply afraid of the truth, her whole life—home, family, job, *literature*—an elaborate construction to keep her from it.

"I hear you," Karla said.

Frankie stared at her sister and mouthed the words without sound, "You do? You hear me?"

"Yes," Karla said, "loud and clear."

As Karla watched Frankie sashay off toward the dartboard and the bowl-cut hair, she felt a tap on her shoulder and turned to see the checkered shirt, and its owner, with wispy blond hair combed back from a large open forehead. His name was Glenn and he described himself as a "schoolteacher-slash-writer," and when he smiled he seemed to age, three deep lines digging into the flesh over his nose.

"I teach too," Karla said. "English Literature at Hunter College."

"My Ph.D's in American Lit," Glenn said. "I applied to over a hundred colleges without getting a single interview." He blinked slowly at her, humbled but seemingly not bitter.

Karla prepared her next words carefully, wanting to encourage him without being condescending. But before she could speak, Frankie came by with news of a party, inviting first Karla, then, not waiting to be introduced, Glenn.

The four of them wedged themselves into the back seat and taxied across the Fifty-Ninth Street Bridge to a renovated warehouse in Queens, where they buzzed in and marched up four flights of stairs to a thick steel door that opened into a huge loft with several large clusters of people and a band at the far end. Frankie spotted a self-service bar and led them to it.

"Shots," Frankie announced, selecting a bottle of tequila and four shot glasses from a silver tray. Lemon and salt were available and she handed each person a wedge of lemon and instructed them to lick the backs of their hands for salt.

"To imperfection," Frankie said, eyeing Karla, and the four of them licked their hands, swallowed the tequila, and sucked the lemons.

After a second round, Frankie led the dart player to the dance floor before the band, Karla and Glenn finding an open sofa.

"Damn," Glenn said, scanning the room, "look at the size of this place," Karla smiling and turning back to watch the dancers.

After several fast songs, the band slowed it down and when most of the couples left the floor, Frankie and the dart player were revealed dancing in the center, their hands hanging at their sides, mouths pressed tightly together. Slowly, Frankie raised her arms over her head as she danced, her whole body writhing against the connection of their mouths, as if caught in an ecstasy of warring impulses.

Back at the bar, Glenn poured another round of shots and with a slack deferential smile, toasted Karla's getting tenure. Setting down her glass, Karla gazed at Glenn through watering eyes, the liquor spreading into her blood, and he leaned forward, his head blocking the overhead light, and kissed her on the lips.

"This one's to good times," Glenn said, pouring another round of shots.

It took Karla two efforts to finish the shot, and when Glenn offered his hand she hesitated, then clasped it in both of hers and followed him toward a distant doorway. Through it, they found a hall, and at its end, an empty bathroom. Inside, Glenn locked the door and, turning back to Karla, offered another wan smile. He stepped over to where Karla leaned against the counter and, holding a firm finger beneath her chin, gazed into her eyes as he unbuttoned her shirt with his other hand. He kissed her mouth and Karla leaned back until her head was against the mirror, peering past the sallow smile into Glenn's eyes.

"Glenn," she said, matching the name to the body. He placed a hand beneath her skirt and slid it up the outside of her thigh. "Glenn," Karla repeated, searching one brown eye then the other, until she noticed a tiny white face peering back at her. Then, as Glen moved in, he closed his eyes, and, disconnected from her own image, Karla felt herself tumbling backward.

Karla didn't feel the mass of her body again until Glenn left her alone and she stood heavily before the mirror reassembling her clothing. She wasn't sure if the weight she felt was groundedness, a settling back down to earth, or if she had fallen from a height she would never regain.

Refusing to get maudlin, she returned to the main room and circulated on her own, pausing before a bookcase of silver-framed photographs in which she couldn't help but note the absence of children and old people. She peered at the flat smiling images.

Across the room, Karla saw Frankie quickly descending a circular iron staircase, the dart player trailing after her but losing ground. Frankie walked briskly across the floor, straight to Karla, and stopped.

"Let's get out of here," Frankie said, and without waiting for either of their dates, the sisters left.

In the taxi, Frankie sat against her door peering out the window as they slid down off the bridge and turned onto a calm, late-night First Avenue. Karla sat against her own door gazing out at the occasional solitary pedestrian and the small groups of men standing before the all-night delis.

"Well," Karla said, "I suppose I should tell you what happened."

"What?" Frankie said dully.

"We had sex in the bathroom."

"Yeah," Frankie said, still peering out her window, "and I knocked off *War and Peace*."

Karla lifted a tired hand. "Swear to God," she said, "I just let it happen."

Frankie turned. "My god, you're serious."

"I am," Karla said heavily, "stone cold serious. How'd it go with the dart player?"

"Karla," Frankie said, "you okay?"

"I'm fine."

Frankie eyed her sister another moment, then shook her head and huffed, turning back to her window. "We go up to this incredible loft, packets of cocaine on the fucking night table," she said, "and he starts wondering how much the party is costing them, how big a mortgage they have." Frankie broke off, shaking her head. "Here we are in fucking *heaven* and he's got to start breaking it all down."

"So the guy wondered how much the place cost," Karla said. "I did too."

"Exactly," Frankie said. "Nobody in this city can have a good time without stopping to analyze it."

At this point, the driver inexplicably turned west, driving a few blocks over and swinging onto Park Avenue, with its two-way traffic a slower route. They pulled up to a red light and Karla was about to question the driver when she noticed, out Frankie's window, the lean figure of a man on the corner shadow boxing.

"Reminds me of Daddy," Karla said.

Frankie located the boxer and the two of them watched the figure, clad in loose-fitting sweats, feint, duck, and release a flurry of short punches.

As the taxi pulled away, Frankie rolled down her window and called out, "Yo, dude!" but the figure didn't react.

Their mother had died when they were children, and their father had retired early and moved them out to an old house overlooking the ocean in Amagansett, the next town in from Montauk. He'd been loving but distant, quietly accepting whatever new decisions the girls made—from Frankie's dropping out of high school to take a Greyhound cross-country to Karla's marrying her English professor, Rob, the summer she finished grad school—before turning back to his endless toil on the house and grounds.

"You know," Karla said, "it's starting to make sense—tonight I mean. Like stepping onto a property past a 'No Trespassing' sign. For a second, you stand there and it's like this big deal, you've broken this huge taboo. But then you just step back off the property."

"What are you talking about?"

"More than anything, I was curious," Karla said.

"People don't fuck because they're curious," Frankie said, and she ordered the driver to stop, opened her door and got out, walking briskly off down the side street. Karla handed the driver a twenty to hold him, and followed.

Frankie stopped and turned back, hair wind-blown, eyes dark. "Take the cab," she said, "I'm walking," and she continued down the block.

"Frankie!" Karla said, catching up, grabbing her sister's arm, "I was saying I *enjoyed* tonight. It was good for me."

"Ooh," Frankie said, facing her, eyes widening, "five seconds on the dark side."

"Stop it," Karla said. "I needed a break, that's all."

"From what? Your tidy little life?"

"From my work, Frankie."

"Spare me," Frankie said. "All you do is write about what other people write about."

"It's *work,* Frankie."

"*You're* work," Frankie huffed, turning again and walking.

Karla again caught and stopped her, this time blocking her path. "What about listening to all your one-week romances?" she said. "And your endless string of complaints? That's not work?"

"It's work because you don't listen, you judge." Frankie attempted to pass, but Karla cut her off.

"I *evaluate*," Karla said. "It's what people do, Frankie. What *adults* do."

Frankie stood motionless, staring back at Karla. The taxi honked from the corner.

"If you're such a fucking adult," Frankie said, "what are you doing out here with me? Why aren't you in Montauk with your husband and daughter?"

"Because, goddammit," Karla said through her teeth, "I have work to do."

"You're just like Dad," Frankie spat, again trying to get past.

"Because I believe in hard work?" Karla said, staying before her.

"Because you don't believe in anything else."

"Talk about judging," Karla said.

Frankie stood still. "I'm telling you what I see. Everything has to fit into your master plan."

Karla hesitated, staring back at Frankie. "Maybe that's what commitment is, what growing up is—*planning*."

The two glared at each other another moment, then Frankie shook her head and stepped over to sit on a low brick wall at the entrance to a building.

Karla released a sigh and sat heavily a few feet away. Each gazed in opposite directions down the empty street. Karla felt shitty for playing the adult card, as she always had. She was about to apologize when Frankie rose and crossed the street, stopping on the far sidewalk and standing still.

Working his way down from the corner, jabbing and feinting, was the shadow boxer. Reaching Frankie, the man slowed to a stop, bouncing on his toes before her, and Frankie slowly raised her fists to her chin, settled herself onto bent knees, and released two probing jabs, poking the air more than punching. The boxer returned two jabs of his own and began to circle, Frankie pivoting, bouncing lightly, throwing a stronger left-right combination. The boxer bobbed low and skipped to the side, Frankie staying with him, throwing another jab, the boxer nimbly twisting and ducking, bracing his back leg, releasing a flurry, and again circling, Frankie turning with him, the two of them rotating in unison, bobbing, feinting, jabbing.

Once Frankie had returned to her spot on the wall, Karla sat listening to the even rhythm of Frankie's panting, thinking about the *pas de deux,* how odd and lovely it had been, how intimate the two of them had seemed, yet also how separate, connected by punches that never landed.

"That was cool," Karla said. "Two total strangers creating your own little drama—your own *opera*."

Frankie looked at Karla as if she didn't understand. "Strangers?" she said.

"I mean, that guy could have been anybody, just jogging down the street in the middle of the night."

"Karla," Frankie said. "That was Jerry Ryan. We used to go out."

Their taxi gone, they walked the three blocks back to First Avenue and hailed another. Out Karla's window, the buildings changed from Irish restaurants to bodegas to chain stores, the city a an odd patchwork that just kept going. Karla wondered what time the earliest Jitney ran to Montauk.

At Frankie's building, Frankie handed Karla a crumpled ten and got out, walking from the light of the street into the darkened entryway. Karla leaned over and lowered the window.

"Why don't you come with me to Montauk?" she called.

"No thanks," came the reply.

Heading west, the taxi crossed Fifth Avenue and slid into Central park. After a few swift turns, a concrete wall rose up beside the car, amplifying the sound of its passage as it descended into the blackness beneath a bridge. Then the taxi seemed to slow, seemed to be stalling there at the nadir, and Karla twisted back to look out the rear window, as if something were there in the darkness grabbing after her. But in the next instant Karla felt the taxi surge upward, and she settled back into place, gazing again through the windshield, into the window of trees and the light of the west side.

Accabonac Harbor

I've had detention four of the last five days, always for talking in class, but with Train sitting next to me, it's just too hard. The teacher starts scratching some formulas on the board and I say, "Why you so long-faced Train dog? Forget your lunch again?"

"Shit," Train says, "I already forgot tomorrow's lunch."

"I got you half a baloney," I tell him.

"You hear about Weasel?" Train says. "Ran away again last night and this morning they found him sleeping in the shed behind the deli. Brought his ass straight to school."

"Why'd he bolt?"

"Getting away from his gonzo pops." Without any warning, Train tilts his head back and sings out, "*Freedom, Freeeeeeedom*!" and the teacher turns back from the board and everyone else turns and looks at him.

But Train just leans over, scribbles intently in his notebook, and the teacher goes back to scratching on that board.

At recess after lunch, I'm trying to cheer up Weasel, telling him to forget about home and go talk to Mary Jane, the girl he's had a crush on for two years but has never spoken to. Weasel raises hell on the soccer field, but off it hardly makes a peep.

"Just be like, 'Yo bitch, what's up?" I tell him.

"Just walk up to her for no reason," Weasel says.

"Don't think about it. Just go."

"Okay, I'm gonna do it," Weasel says, and he turns and walks straight over to Mary Jane Riley. She sees him approaching and shifts her weight to one foot, crosses her arms. He marches straight up to her and stops. Mary Jane's face goes sour and I'm thinking oh no, what the hell are you saying, Weasel.

Weasel walks back to me with a half smile on his face, looking proud and shame-faced at the same time.

"What did you say?" I ask him.

"I said, 'Yo bitch, what's up?'"

"You called her 'bitch'?"

"Yeah."

"Damn," I say.

Next day at lunch, Weasel slogs over to where I'm sitting with Train and a couple others. He sits down and makes a millisecond of eye contact, then looks down at his sandwich and eats.

Train goes up to buy some milk and I say to Weasel, "Today you say something different. To Mary Jane or to somebody else. Doesn't matter who."

"Nah," Weasel says, looking down. "I'm cool."

"You are not cool," I say. "You are hang-dog mopey. Yesterday you were cool. You walked up to the hottest chick in school and called her bitch."

"I was so freakin' scared, I didn't even know what I was saying."

"Exactly. You are the man, Weasel. You are the boss."

Weasel looks up at me, trying to gauge if I'm serious or busting his balls.

"Yesterday you took names, dude."

"They think I'm a creep," he says.

"They don't know what to think. You calling one of them bitch—they can't even process that. Today you go over to 'em and *you* tell *them* what it means. Feel me?"

"You mean explain what I meant?"

"No. Move on to the next chapter. That's the thing about doing stupid shit—trust me, I know what I'm talking about here—people can't figure it out so you just keep going, stay one step ahead of 'em."

"I could tell her I didn't mean it," Weasel says.

"Forward dude, forward."

Train sits down, chugs his carton of milk, and places it on the table next to four other empties.

"Yo Train, what should Weasel say to Mary Jane?"

"Not what he said yesterday," Train says.

"You gotta be like, 'Yesterday?'" I say to Weasel, "I can't even *remember* yesterday. Yesterday *who*? motherfuckers."

"Like I don't even care if it was stupid," Weasel says.

"Like you the man and the rest of us is all children," Train says.

Weasel turns back, looks toward the other tables in the lunchroom.

"What you got to lose?" Train says. "What do any of us have to lose?"

Train looks around the room and I say "Easy, big guy," seeing he's getting one of his urges. The lunch lady has her back to us, solving a problem at the cash register.

Train stands up, steps onto his chair, then jumps up onto the table, both of his big-ass work boots landing square in the middle, spreads his arms and shouts up at the ceiling, "Take me now, Lord! Put me out of my misery!"

I grab him by his belt, and he jumps back to the ground as the entire room breaks into applause, the lunch lady turning too late to see what happened, and the bell rings ending lunch.

When I walk into his office, Dr. Peabody waits a second for full dramatic effect, then spins around in his high-backed chair and lowers his glasses to the tip of his nose. The guy's like thirty years old but goes for the senior doctor, wise old sage effect.

"Jab," he says, "how's it going?"

"Great," I say.

"Tell me. What's going on that's great?"

"You know," I say, "regular stuff."

"'Regular' is not 'great,'" he says.

"That's your opinion," I say.

He looks at me for a minute. "Okay," he says, "then everything in your life is absolutely terrific, as good as it could be. Nothing could be better."

"Yep," I say. "Except for maybe one thing."

"And what's that?"

"School."

"What's not great about school?"

"Period 1," I say, "period 2, period 3, period 4, period 5—no period 5 is lunch—period 6, period 7, and period 8."

"So what are you going to do about it?" Peabody says.

"Nothing," I say.

"Sounds rather passive."

"What *can* I do?"

"If you're given lemons . . ." he begins.

"We tried to form a rap group," I tell him, "but as soon as they heard a bad word they shut us down."

"What word?" He's always telling me it's okay to speak openly, anything goes.

"Guess," I say.

"F bomb?"

"A compound form of it."

"Mother F?" he says.

"See?" I say. "You think it's bad too."

"No I don't."

"Then say it."

"Motherfucker," he says, looking straight at me.

"Very good," I say. "But now you've got to go do like a week of volunteer work or something."

"Bullshit," he says.

"Oooo," I say, "now you gotta do two weeks."

"Piss-ass," he says.

"That's weak," I say, "you're losing it."

"Bitchwhore," he says with a stupid grin.

"First of all," I say, "if you're gonna put two words together, they can't be like, whatchamacallit, when you say the same word twice."

"Synonyms," he says.

"When they repeat the same meaning."

"Redundant."

"You don't say 'dickdong,' but maybe 'dickbrain.' Not 'Assbutt' but 'ass*fuck*.'"

"Gotcha," he says.

"Or shitmouth," I say.

"Wo," he says.

"Cumface," I say. "Cuntstain."

"Damn," Peabody says, "you're like a fountain."

When our time is up, old Peabody looks at the clock like he does at the end of every session, like he hates to have to end it, stands up, shakes my hand, and says to take it easy, and I'm wondering how the poor guy is going to make it through the next week till I come back.

As soon as I walk through the main door half way through period one, the greeter tells me the principal, Mr. Pivro, wants to see me in his office. My first feeling is "Oh shit," which is quickly followed by "Okay, whatever," followed by "Fuck him." Peabody says my brain is springloaded. Push me one way, I'll push back the other way twice as hard.

I walk down the empty hallway, first period well under way. Pivro's assistant tells me to sit down but before I can, Pivro's door swings open.

"Good morning, Mr. Parker," he says, and waves me in.

I sit in the green plastic chair across from his desk.

"We received a report from a parent about some texts that contained threats," he says.

He looks at me with raised eyebrows, giving me a chance to say something. But I have no idea what he's referring to. I send about 500 texts a day—every night I lie in bed and text for hours and on any given night threaten pretty much everyone I know with everything I can think of, from punches in the balls to cooking their cats.

"I didn't threaten anyone," I say. This is my reflex. I don't think, I just deny.

"Give yourself a moment," Pivro says. "It will be better if you come clean."

"Last night, I didn't even have my phone," I say, digging in.

"Where did you leave it?" Pivro says.

"In the locker room."

Pivro lifts the receiver off his desk phone, checks a number on a sheet, and dials. He rolls his eyes up to the ceiling as he listens, and a couple seconds later I hear a buzz coming from my backpack. I forgot to silence it.

"You want to answer that?" Pivro says.

"I don't take calls in school," I say, and he hangs up the phone.

"Jab," Pivro says, "who did you text last night?"

"Weasel, Train," I say, accepting defeat for the last round and gearing up for the next. "Maybe a couple others."

"And what did you say to Weasel?"

"Same thing I always say. School sucks."

"Anything else?"

"I told him he shouldn't take his old man's crap anymore. Told him if his old man messes with him again, he should take a board and go upside his head."

"There we go," Pivro says. Then he leans forward onto his elbows and says, "All threats are supposed to be reported to the police. But instead, I'm giving you detention after school today, then a two-day in-school suspension. Detention hall after school today, and first thing tomorrow, report to the counseling office."

"What about Weasel? What's happening to him?"

"Same thing," Pivro says. "He'll serve his in-school detention on the other side of the school, in the nurse's office."

"I need you to make better decisions," my old man says that night at dinner, after telling me he got a call from Pivro.

We are sitting at the table together, a rarity. Usually it's just me eating a Hungry Man or frozen pizza, him in the den watching the news.

My father and mother split when I was 8. I didn't care then and don't now. Everybody wants me to care but I don't. That's their business. My mom lives right next door so I see her plenty, and my dad, well he's always telling me how he *needs* me to do stuff.

"I mean it," he says. "I need you to take responsibility for your actions."

"Fine," I say, forking some freshly nuked turkey into my mouth.

"You know," my dad says, "I had some troubles in school too."

He likes to tell me how he got off to a rough start in life but worked hard to overcome it.

"I would have dropped out of ninth grade if I'd been able to," he says. He shifts his eyes from me up to the far corner of the ceiling, thinking about the bad old days. “Me and my buddies started skipping school, just hanging out, living out on the edges.”

“That was when you hitchhiked to Iowa,” I say. Once a year or so, he comes back to the hitching cross-country story.

“Me and Jimmy Orosco,” he says. “Made it to Ames, Iowa. Trucker dropped us in this little park downtown where we met other runaways, *real* runaways, kids with no intention of ever going back.”

“You camped out with them.”

“Three nights. Owner of a hardware store had a shed in the back he cleared out to make a barracks, with a porta potty behind it and a hose to drink and wash. Girls and boys, they all sprayed each other down, then wrapped up in these army blankets the guy gave them. Every night at dark, they'd all come back.”

“But one got taken away.”

“Kid named Dust. Set up this fortune telling table with a couple others and gave readings for donations. They made these beautiful cards—Hope cards, they called them.

“The third day we were there,” he says, “the police came to the table and took Dust away—his family must have tracked him down—and he looked back at us—Jimmy and I were hanging out cause Dust's partner at the table was kind of sweet—he just looked back at us and goes, ‘Tell everybody it'll be okay,’ and they put him in the back of the cruiser.”

My dad looks at me. “The point,” he says, “is that living out there was rough for these kids. They had to scratch and claw for every scrap of food, just to be warm at night.”

“Sounds like going back was worse,” I say.

The next day I go straight to the nurse's office, see Weasel sitting in the adjoining room with the cot, but the nurse tells me I'm supposed to go to Counseling. Having scored an alibi for some extra time, I take the long way through the halls. My usual preference is to hit the bathroom, sit in one of the stalls and listen to music. Sometimes, I'll shimmy out the bathroom window, walk down to the deli for a drink, or head the other way, through the horse farm to Accabonac Harbor.

Passing the art room, I see Train at the table near the door sketching something, slip in and sit at his table till the teacher sees me and kicks me out.

I head down to Counseling and into Ms. Elliot's office, set my old decoy cell phone on her desk and sit at the small table. Once Ms. Elliot gets busy working, I remove my good cell phone from my pocket and, beneath the table, text Weasel.

We bullshit back and forth for about twenty minutes, then meet in the bathroom by the auditorium. We do chin-ups in the stalls, slap box, travel around the entire room without touching the ground, climbing from sink to sink, climbing over the first stall, onto the toilet, over the next stall, onto the radiator, wedge ourselves between the ceiling and the hand dryers, and complete the circuit with a long final step back onto the sink.

I wander back to Counseling and after playing games on my phone for a half hour or so, Ms. Elliot takes a call and tells me to go to Pivro's office. I walk to the far corridor, turn into Pivro's suite, and sit in the waiting chair by the secretary.

Pivro's door opens and red-faced puffy-eyed Mary Jane rushes past me avoiding eye contact. I wonder what I did this time.

"Come in, Jab."

He tells me that yesterday afternoon, Mary Jane received upsetting texts from me and asks if I'd like to tell him what I said. I say not really. He then pushes his notepad over so I can see what he wrote.

> Jab: Yo ho, why you dissin my boy Weasel?
>
> Mary Jane: Why do you always have to act so cocky?
>
> Jab: I can't help it if I have a big cock.

"It's two things," Pivro says, "first, what you said, and second, the texts were sent during your after-school detention. I'm giving you two more days."

I shrug.

"You are not to do anything during detentions. Why is that so hard for you, Jab? Why is it so hard for you to simply do nothing?"

"Beats me," I say.

"Now go back to the counseling office and do nothing," Pivro says. "*Nothing*. Got it?"

"Maybe if I could listen to music," I say, "it'd be easier not to, you know, get into trouble."

"You are missing the point," Pivro says.

"How about doodling in my notebook? Can I at least do that?"

"*Nothing,*" he says.

Walking back down the long dim hall to the counseling office, I feel like shit, like a fish that every time it starts to swim away gets reeled back into the boat.

Then I walk into the counseling office, seal my lips, go to my chair, sit still and stare at the wall.

I do nothing for a solid five minutes, no exaggeration, at least doubling my previous best time. For five full minutes I stare straight at the wall—don't slouch over, don't look around, *nothing*. But then I start feeling queasy, then faint, like I'm going to pass out, and I tell Ms. Elliot I'm not feeling well.

"Rough morning, huh?" she says.

"I better go to the bathroom," I say.

"Go ahead," she says.

I head down the hall, passing the near bathroom and heading to the one in the far wing. I walk in and straight to the window on the far wall, wind it open, slither out, and drop the five or so feet to the ground.

I head toward Accabonac Harbor, staying far away from the horses as I cross through the corral, find a grassy patch and sit looking out at the blue water. An egret stands about fifty yards away perfectly still, and my first impulse is to shout out and make it flee, but I just suck in a breath and watch it. After a minute I lean back on the ground and look up at the sky.

I just lie there and watch the thin clouds wisping past.

But then, just like that, my stomach fills with dread, and I realize the moment is over. I pick myself up and walk back to school.

DRY SEASON

They hadn't had rain of any significance in six weeks, and although Jonathan and Sarah had sustained the small vegetable garden in back, the lawn was now a lost cause. They'd left the city five years earlier, Sarah working remotely as a technical writer, and Jonathan, an architectural draftsman, splitting his time between home and the new office in Sag Harbor. Although children had always been part of the plan, the subject hadn't come up in a while. So when they heard a honk the Thursday afternoon beginning the long July 4th weekend, first Sarah ran outside, then Jonathan, each of them leaning in to shake Merrill's hand and get a look at who sat beside him.

Seeing Geena, whom they'd met during Merrill's visit last fall, Jonathan stepped back, put his arm around Sarah's waist, and said dinner was on him.

Waiting for Merrill and Geena to drop their bags and shower three doors down, Jonathan added the last of the mulch to the faltering rose bushes and Sarah finished cutting back the four hydrangeas wrapping around the corner of the house no longer able to flower.

"Cool he's still with Geena," Jonathan called over.

"Best thing that ever happened to him," Sarah answered.

"I had a feeling something was up when he bought that membership to MOMA," Jonathan said.

"Where my dick leads, there shall I follow," Sarah said.

"Oooh," Jonathan said, "you feeling frisky?"

"Almost," said Sarah. "I'm *almost* feeling frisky."

The two couples met in town for an early movie, women sitting in the middle, and afterward grabbed a table at Cittá Nuova, ordering cocktails and agreeing the movie'd been a disappointment.

"I'll take a crappy movie out here over a great one in the city anytime," Merrill said.

"Eh," Geena said. "I like it out here, but not to the point of enjoying bad movies."

With olive skin and green eyes, thick hair that extended in a bunch to her shoulders, Geena was more effusive, less cautious, than Merrill's previous girlfriends.

The waiter took their order for a second round of drinks, and Jonathan ordered calamari and a large Caprese salad for the table, Geena adding in a melodious Italian, "*E pane per favore*," the waiter smiling and nodding.

"You're Italian?" Jonathan said. "I thought you were middle eastern or something."

"You thought," Sarah groaned, "she was Mediterranean."

"Neither," Geena said.

The busboy delivered the water and filled their water glasses, and as they ate, Jonathan took notice of how solicitous Merrill had become, buttering a piece of bread and handing it to Geena, and watched for Geena to reciprocate, exchanging a pleased look with Sarah when she wiped a crumb from his shirt and kissed him on the cheek.

"What do you do in the city?" Sarah asked Geena.

"Work at a design company downtown," Geena said. "I'm an intern."

"She just knocks on their door and a few minutes later is in there drawing up plans," Merrill said.

"Maybe take a look at our place," Sarah said. She rolled her eyes toward Jonathan. "Tell the hubby it's time to replace the parents' furniture."

"That furniture's worth over a hundred grand," Jonathan said.

"Because its antique," Sarah said. "Meant to be sold, or exhibited, not sat in."

"Oh no!" Geena cried out, clutching at her neck, Jonathan and Sarah momentarily alarmed. "I can't breathe, but I can't take off this manacle because it's made of gold!"

"Guilty as charged," Jonathan said and they all clinked glasses.

The waiter delivered the plate of calamari and, as the busboy topped off their water glasses, asked if they were ready to order dinner. They decided to stay with appetizers.

"Oysters," Jonathan suggested. "And vino."

The waiter recommended a couple of whites, but they settled on a light red Lambrusco.

"Vabbene," Geena said to the waiter, *"uno bottiglia e due dozzina di ostriche, per favore."*

"You keep talking like that," Jonathan said, "we won't need the oysters."

"I always need them!" Geena said, laughing, leaning against Merrill.

"I doubt it," Jonathan said.

Sarah gave Jonathan a look. "So where did you grow up?" she asked Geena.

"Brooklyn," Geena said. "Born and raised."

"People still speak Italian in Brooklyn?" Jonathan said.

"I spent two years in the Italian Alps, in Sondrio, where my mother's from."

"Lucky you," Sarah said.

"Helped soften the landing when my parents split."

"Your dad's from New York?" Sarah asked.

"Oh yeah," Geena said.

Geena was thirty-two, eight years younger than Merrill, and after high school had spent a year in art school before dropping out to go backpacking abroad.

"Ever since I read this story in eleventh grade about the blue men,'" she said, "I wanted to go to Morocco and see the Bedouin."

"So did you?" Sarah said.

"I trekked through the desert with one."

"What's this?" Merrill said.

"Amastan. Met him at the market my first day in Fez."

"Was he gorgeous?" Sarah asked.

"Did he bathe?" asked Jonathan.

The waiter came by, emptying the wine bottle into their glasses and going for another.

"Turned out he wasn't even Bedouin," Geena said. "Had a trust fund, an apartment downtown, just couldn't deal with people, so he'd made a break. Just him and his two camels. And for six weeks, me."

"What did you do all day?" Sarah asked.

"Schlepped from camp to camp checking his water contraptions, these huge screens that collected water from fog and dew his family'd built for the herders."

"Fog in the desert?" Jonathan said.

"Wherever there's groundwater," Geena said. "Amastan would wake me out of a dead sleep—'Time for the water'—and we'd head off to collect the jugs, load up the camels, and deliver them to the camps of nomads."

"And I thought I was worldly," Sarah said, "spending a night with a bicycle messenger in Barcelona."

"Half a night," Jonathan said, turning to the others. "The guy's bed was too small so she bailed."

"I would have bailed," Geena said. "Here's this guy living in the Sahara, most austere place in the world . . ."

"What?" Sarah said.

"All he wanted to talk about was America, asking about Hollywood, Miami Beach. The last two weeks we were hardly speaking."

"Sounds like things cooled off in the tent," Jonathan said.

Sarah released a loud sigh, reached over and slid Jonathan's wine away from him, Jonathan immediately grabbing it and sliding it back.

Seeing their lawn-care guy, Daryl, enter with his brother Jaylen, Jonathan stood up and intercepted them before they reached their table on the opposite side, the others looking on as Jonathan shook hands and exchanged bro hugs with each.

"Daryl mows what's left of our lawn," Sarah explained as Jonathan returned to the table. "Local guy, been cutting grass since he was ten years old. Now he's got three trucks, and what—" she turned to Jonathan—"five guys working for him?"

"That other guy his partner?" Merrill asked.

"Brother," Jonathan said. "Helps out once in a while, but he's got some issues."

"I don't like him," Sarah said.

"He's okay," Jonathan said. 'Daryl told me about some nasty shit they went through growing up."

"This world's got plenty of nasty," Merrill said, glancing at Geena who was thumbing her phone. "But it's cool you guys are friends."

"Plantation friends," Sarah said. "Black people go to white people's homes as employees, cutting the grass, caring for the children, and the white people say they're friends."

"I've always wondered," Jonathan said, "if black folks weren't actually better off. You know, being locked out of the big house, excluded from our materialist frenzy."

"Oh yes," Sarah said, "being excluded offers so many advantages."

Geena looked up from her phone. "My father was black," she said.

"Black like how?" Jonathan said.

"*How*?" Sarah said. "How are you white?"

"Inner-city black, suburban black, international black?" Jonathan said.

"He did time," Geena said.

"Time how?" Jonathan said. "I'm serious—" he raised a hand to keep Sarah from interrupting—"'cause he was trapped in the 'hood feeling hopeless or some sort of white collar criminal?"

"Trapped," Geena said.

Returning from the bathroom, Jonathan detoured over to Daryl's table and exchanged another round of hand-shakes before returning to the table where Sarah paused mid-sentence as he sat.

"So yes," Sarah continued, "I wanted children. The thing is, the *marriage* has to want them."

"I have an uncle," Merrill said. "We called him Uncle Cash, 'cause he was always doling out twenties to my brother and me, and he used to say, 'I love kids. Other people's kids!'"

"Listen," Jonathan said, not looking at Sarah but speaking to her, "if the clock runs out, there's always adoption."

"Sure," Sarah said, "go down to Costco and pick out a child. Or maybe a puppy." She turned to the others. "At one point, he actually said that, 'How about we get a puppy?'"

"I didn't say a kid *or* a puppy," Jonathan said.

"No," Sarah said, "just a puppy."

Wine glasses sitting empty, Jonathan was about to request the check when two young couples entered the dining room in a whirlwind of excitement, laughing, talking loudly, as if it were an amazing stroke of good fortune that they had found a room with open tables. As the waiter returned from taking their drink order, Jonathan signaled for another bottle of wine.

"I'd like to have a beautiful little girl," Geena said.

"You got a father picked out?" Merrill said.

"I'd like to *have* one," Geena said, "not grow one inside me." She held her glass aloft for the waiter to fill. "She'd have green eyes and brown hair streaked with blonde in the summer. Like mine at Long Beach."

"I used to go to the summer concerts at Long Beach," Jonathan said.

"My mother's family had a cottage where the three of us would spend the summer," Geena said, "my dad working in the city, taking three-day weekends. On Friday morning, I'd lay in bed listening until I'd hear his voice boom through the house: 'Go ahead and fire me! I'm going to the beach with my girl!'"

The busboy stopped by to top off their waters, Merrill lifting his glass, taking a swallow.

"Ah," he said, "straight from the fog collector."

"On Monday morning he'd be gone," Geena said. "In the evening my mom and I would be out in the yard playing badminton or sitting on the patio drinking Shirley Temples, and he'd come strolling down the street in his oil-stained uniform."

"Did they get along?" Sarah asked.

"At the beach they did. But my dad's life was in the city."

"You can take the boy out of the city . . ." Merrill said.

"What'd he do time for?" Jonathan asked.

"Skimming cash."

"Because they didn't pay him enough!" Sarah blurted.

Geena took a sip of wine, the others waiting. "The first summer without him, I was twelve—they split before he got busted—and it was like, I don't know, the house was just so quiet."

Sarah turned to Jonathan.

"I'm not saying it was sad," Geena said.

"Sometimes sad up front is better than bad later," Jonathan said.

"Which are we?" Sarah said to Jonathan.

"Neither," he said.

"Ah yes," Geena said, "the third option." She leaned over, planted a kiss on Merrill's cheek, and excused herself to use the bathroom.

"She misses him," Sarah said.

"You should see the portrait she hung in our living room," Merrill said. "Him standing in a doorway looking back at you over his shoulder. Creeps me out."

"Her way of keeping him around," Sarah said. "Why don't you have any pictures of your mother?" she said to Jonathan.

"I do," Jonathan said. "Small ones. In a photo album."

"About this third option," Jonathan said, once Geena had returned. "Yes, Sarah and I have decided to live a certain way. And maybe there's some regret, some sadness, not having kids. I mean, of course there is. But you've got to keep moving forward."

"What's the third option?" Merrill asked.

"Something between sadness and badness," Sarah said.

"Not caring," Geena said.

"Yes," Jonathan said, gazing at Geena, "numbness. The crater crusting over and forming a thick calloused skin. But then, look at that!" He slapped the table with both palms. "Where there was a hole, we now have a dance floor! You like to dance, Geena?"

Sarah shook her head and groaned.

"I told them about the picture of your dad," Merrill said to Geena.

Geena took a swallow of wine, raised her eyes, gazing past the others. "One minute, we're playing on the beach," she said, "and the next, he's like, 'It was good while it lasted!'"

"Jesus," Sarah said.

"No, no," Geena said, looking at Sarah, "it was how it had to be. That same week I had my first boyfriend, and then it was off to Sondrio."

"One door closes, other doors open," Jonathan said.

Geena reached an arm around Merrill's shoulders. "And now I've got this guy."

"You know I'll never walk out," Merrill said.

"Yes I do," Geena said.

The waiter came by and suggested an aperitif.

"Coffee," Jonathan said.

Geena raised a finger. "*Con latte per favore.*"

Merrill said he'd have the same, and Sarah shook her head.

The busboy delivered the cups and set down a small pitcher of cream as the waiter poured the coffee.

"Sometimes when I'd misbehave," Geena said, again raising her eyes, "he'd glare at me with this twinkle in his eye and bellow out, 'This nigga might have to kick some ass today!'"

"The man had a sense of irony," Jonathan said.

"Irony?" Sarah said.

"Being a black dude from the city hanging out with a white chick at Long Beach."

"How's that ironic?" Sarah said.

"Because he knew it couldn't last," Jonathan said.

"Of course it could have," Sarah said. "We know mixed couples."

"Barry and Linda?" Jonathan said. "She's hardly black."

Sarah stared at him. "*What*?"

"He means not culturally black," Geena said.

"Whereas your dad," Jonathan said to Geena, "that dude was *black*."

"Is," Sarah corrected.

"Black as night," Geena said, eying Jonathan.

"Black as coal," Jonathan returned.

"Black as the hole in my heart," Geena said, eyes flaring.

Sarah tipped back her wine glass and drained what was left, holding it to her lips an extra second before setting the glass down and turning to Jonathan.

"You don't like parenting and you don't like parents," she said.

"I like Sarah's dad," Jonathan said.

"You like the painting of her dad," Sarah said

"Hey," Jonathan said, glancing at Geena, "it was good while it lasted!"

"But it didn't have to end," Sarah said. She turned to Geena. "Why not call him, invite him out for a weekend?"

"Don't know his number," Geena said.

"Your mother must have it," Sarah said.

Geena smiled and shook her head doubtfully.

"He doesn't want to come out here," Jonathan said.

"We'll help you find him," Sarah continued. "Track down his old friends."

"Sarah," Jonathan said.

"There must be a way."

"Sarah, stop."

Sarah turned to Geena. "But what if you have children?" she said. "He'll want to see them, won't he?"

"Children?" Geena said.

"If you and Merrill—if you and anyone, decide to have them."

"Sarah," Jonathan said.

Geena gazed at Sarah. "If we decide to?" she said.

"Yes! You'll get a little older and you'll be ready for it to be about somebody else."

Geena gazed back at Sarah, narrowing her eyes, trying to understand. Then she lifted her chin, located the waiter across the room, and sang out, *"Signore, piú vino per favore!"*

Merrill took Geena in his arm. "I got my little girl right here," he said.

The bus boy gone for the night, the table was strewn with napkins and empty glasses. The two young couples finished their drinks and quietly left.

The waiter came by and Jonathan slipped a credit card into the check holder, handed it to him, then raised his water glass to his lips, drained the last few drops, and lowered it to the table.

When the waiter returned the check holder, only Geena was sitting upright, Merrill slumping beside her, one arm looped over Geena's forearm, Jonathan leaning on an elbow, Sarah slinking low at his side, scrolling through pictures on her phone.

"Time to get the car," Geena said to Merrill. "I'll meet you out front."

Hoisting himself to a stand, Merrill first shook Jonathan's hand, then leaned down and kissed Sarah on the cheek, Sarah blinking and smiling.

"Thanks for dinner," Merrill said, and off he went.

Geena located her bag and straightened herself, sitting erect in her seat as if steeling herself for whatever came next.

Jonathan scooched his chair closer to Sarah, so that their armrests touched, Sarah letting her head fall against his shoulder.

"Merrill's a good dude," Jonathan said to Geena.

"He absolutely adores you," Sarah said, regaining her voice.

Geena stood up and slung her bag over a shoulder. "Merrill will be fine," she said.

Geena smoothed the wrinkles from her sweater with both hands, Jonathan and Sarah sitting low in their chairs, watching.

"You all will be," she said, planting a heel and spinning away in a tidy pirouette.

Freetown

Shooting hoops at the court behind the Presbyterian church, I noticed an old blue Taurus wagon, and inside a dark figure watching. A few days later, the same car pulled in and Lance Williams, the star of the high school team who lived in Freetown, East Hampton's black section, got out.

"I heard about some backwards-dunking white boy," he said.

We chose for the ball and played dead even until point game, when Lance backed me toward the basket, then stepped back, and drained a jump-shot before I could even leave my feet.

"Good game," he said.

"Yeah," I said, slapping his hand.

He walked through the gate, the back of his shirt dark with sweat, then turned back, looking through the chain-link fence.

"I've seen you in school," he said. "You don't say much."

"Guess not," I said.

"Well," he said, "maybe there ain't nothing *to* say." And he walked off to his car.

~

In school, Lance talked me into going out for the team, and two weeks later we were matched up in scrimmages, both of us 6’ 2”, him the star, me the newcomer, the only other kid with skills and above-the-rim hops. After he scored on me, he’d say, “Aw, come on now.” Then I’d bust him back, and he’d smile and wink. “Yeah,” he’d say, “that fire starting to come out.”

We won our first game, Lance scoring twenty, me nineteen, and afterward I rode with Lance, leaving my bike chained to the rack, and we cruised Main Street, then drove the long loop, hitting all the beaches on the bay side before swinging over to the ones on the ocean. Not mentioning the game, Lance just wanted to drive, from one beach to the next. By the time we got pulled over, I was nearly asleep.

“What’s going on, officer?” Lance said rolling down his window.

“Where you fellas headed?” the cop said.

“Just driving,” Lance said.

“Where to?”

“Nowhere,” Lance said.

“You been drinking?”

“Did I do something wrong?”

“Routine check.”

“My ass,” Lance muttered.

“What’s that?” The cop leaned in the window.

I thought it might help if the cop saw me, and I leaned over. “We had a game tonight,” I said.

The cop looked from me back to Lance. “Guess you just never learned your manners,” he said, and returned to his cruiser.

We pulled in the first driveway after the Freetown trailer park, beside a small, shingled house, and Lance shut off the motor.

“You believe that cop?” he said.

“Trying to break the boredom,” I said.

“It ain’t boredom, Ricky.”

“Whatever.” I opened the door, ready to go inside.

“If that’s how you feel, okay,” Lance said. “But don’t come over my house and tell me the dude is pulling me over, telling me mind my manners because he’s bored.”

I pulled my door closed and sat there watching our breath fog the windshield, feeling like I’d been pulled into a trap.

“So what’s this ‘breaking the boredom’?” Lance said.

“He’s just some cop with nothing better to do than mess with a couple of high school kids.”

“He wasn’t messing with you, Ricky.”

I didn’t respond, just sat there, the windows completely fogged, wondering how long it would take to walk home.

“You gonna say anything?” Lance said finally.

“Sometimes,” I said, “there ain’t nothing *to* say.”

The next day at practice Lance and I kept our distance. Then, when we scrimmaged, I caught an outlet pass and angled toward the basket, only Lance having a chance to stop me. Sensing an edge, I figured what the hell, cocked the ball in my right hand as I leaped, and slammed it down through the hoop.

Only once I'd landed and turned to run back up the court did I see where Lance had stopped a few feet short of the basket, never even bothering to jump. And though I was pumped from throwing it down off a dead run, the thrill was cheapened by Lance just letting me go.

"Nice effort," I said, trotting back up court.

"What's that?" Lance said, catching up to me, both of us stopping and facing each other.

"You just gave up," I said.

"It's a scrimmage," he said. "Who gives a shit?"

Coach called us from the other end of the court.

"So just fuck it, right?" I said to Lance. "Fuck everything."

"Right," he said.

"Cause your shit is too thick to crawl out of," I said, the words surprising him and, I guess, me too.

His body tightened, shoulders straightening, and he stepped up close, bringing his face to within a few inches of mine. I didn't back up, just stared into his hardened eyes.

"It's true," I said, words coming I'd never even thought. "You're stuck in your own shit."

Lance swung quickly, his fist connecting with the bridge of my nose, sending me reeling back. I straightened up and blinked to clear my eyes.

"And now," I said, "you're a nigger throwing punches."

Lance swung again but this time I ducked, and before he could get off another punch the other players had reached us, two of them holding him back. Coach asked us who had started it and we both said simultaneously, "He did."

Then, looking at Lance, thinking back over the last two months, back to when he walked out on the court behind the church, I decided he was right. He may have sought me out, may have drawn me in, but the words I spoke were all mine.

"I did," I said to Coach, then looked at Lance. "You happy now?" I said.

"Yeah," he said, and turned and walked away. Then he stopped and turned back. "Turns out you *do* have something to say," he said.

But I just stood there looking at him, saying nothing, watching him turn again and walk off across the gym, the expanse between us widening, the curve of the earth itself rising up into the hard shining floor.

Highway 216

Having booked a one-bedroom suite within a quarter mile of the university where Janet's nephew would be graduating, they decided to leave the car at the Orient Point ferry and once they boarded the train in New London, their five year old, Stevie, able to wander the aisle, Janet and Rob taking turns walking up and back with their snuggly-bound five-month old, they were glad they did.

Two hours later, they taxied through the historic Springburg downtown, past the stone wall entrance to the university, and turned from Main Street onto Highway 216, into the commercial district, the driver, unable to turn left into the hotel, continuing on and turning at the next light into a shopping center, circumnavigating the huge parking lot, and returning to backtrack along 216.

The hotel was clean and quiet, the woman at the desk friendly, though a bit taken aback to hear they had arrived sans auto.

"What'd you come by parachute?" she said.

"Taxi from the train station," Rob said.

"Where's there a train station?" the woman said.

"Bainbridge," Rob said. He looked to Janet for help. "What'd it take from the train station, Jan, fifteen minutes?"

"If that," Janet said, busy refilling the baby's bottle from her nylon shoulder bag. "Easy peasy."

The one-bedroom King Suite on the third floor had more than enough room, with two TVs and a large window in the bedroom that looked out over the highway and the rooftop of the Cineplex 12 across the way, all the way to a line of misty grey mountains in the distance.

Released from the constraints of travel, Stevie raced up and down the third floor corridor, then came in and wrestled with his father on the King bed until Rob, casting an apologetic glance at Janet, said that because this was a vacation, Stevie should be given a little extra TV time.

Janet gave him a look—the rule was to never offer Stevie an exception without first clearing it with the other parent. Still, she conceded with a nod, this was a vacation.

Rob worked as the Sag Harbor Village Bookkeeper, and Janet taught second grade, though she was taking a full year of leave with the new baby, which had not been planned. "Wanted, just not expected," was how Janet liked to put it.

The plan had been to have the second one earlier, when Stevie was two, certainly no later than three, but Rob had gone through some trouble at work. A tax overcharge to more than half the commercial properties in Sag Harbor had been attributed to faulty bookkeeping, until finally, nine months later, an investigator hired by the county tracked the problem to the Assessor's office. At which point, Stevie about to turn three, they tried but couldn't get pregnant.

"It might take a while for your little guys to get strong again," Janet had said after reporting, for the fifth consecutive month, that her period had come.

Feeling baited, Rob managed not to respond. Whereas during their first few years of marriage, he had been unable to hold fire after any slight, more recently he had found that, a lot like the desire for something sweet after dinner, if you just ignore the urge, *poof*, it goes away.

And so they entered Stevie in pre-school and Janet returned to her 2nd grade classroom that looked out on the school's courtyard with its stone birdbath and monument to whalers lost at sea, and the first Sunday morning of November, the morning after a night of too much wine, capped off by a sloppy encounter in bed, into which Rob had coaxed Janet from the maudlin state that always followed her third glass, Janet woke up feeling a faint flutter deep within and, at first, a sense of gratitude that their family plan was back on track, but then immediately afterward, a wave of misgiving.

"Of course you feel doubt," Rob had said when, after the test came back positive, Janet had described her mixed feelings. "You're going to have a baby. Our family is going to be bigger."

Rob's need to state the obvious always irked Janet. "You're going to school, Stevie boy, and I'm going to work!" he'd announce for no reason, clapping his hands after eating his morning bowl of Cheerios, as if he needed to skip ahead, corral the events of the next moment rather than let them unfold on their own. Even cooking Sunday breakfast, he'd offer a forecast of his own imminent actions: "Going to get out the eggs, get out the cheese, and make some omelets!"

That evening they had Chinese delivered to the hotel, read aloud some books they'd brought for Stevie, then tucked him in on the fold-out sofa in the living area and put the baby down in a smother-free safe zone they constructed in the middle of their king bed. The baby sleeping soundly between them, Rob cast Janet a conspiratorial glance and switched from the History channel to a buddy-cop movie on HBO, venturing out to the vending machine at the hall's end, tip-toing back into the bedroom, hands behind his back, and proffering two bags of Famous Amos mini chocolate chip cookies

"Oh, Amos," Janet said, lifting a bag from Rob's palm, "where have you been?"

In the morning, Rob woke first and went down to the breakfast room, finding a plastic cereal dispenser containing Fruit Loops and Frosted Flakes, a beverage dispenser containing Orange and Apple drink with 5% natural fruit juice, and a waffle station with pumps for eight different syrups.

He resisted the urge to grab a quick waffle, one of the family saws being, "Sugar *after* meals, not during," and went to the front desk to ask about nearby options for breakfast.

The guy at the desk was tall and slim with a thick mustache—looked more like a truck driver than a hotel clerk. "We got plenty," he said. "IHOP, Denny's, you name it."

"Any local places?" Rob asked.

"They're all local," said the man.

"I mean locally owned. Non-chain."

"Let me tell you something," the guy said, leaning forward with both elbows on the counter. "Some of them places could be owned by anyone. I mean, they got people in 'em I guarantee you've never seen anywhere else."

"Back in the day, I bet you knew everyone in town," Rob said.

"Not everyone," the guy said. "But you'd *see* everyone. Nowadays you only see some, and most of them, you never see again."

The clerk raised his eyebrows conspiratorially, and Rob shrugged.

"Take one of these," the man said, handing Rob a small card. "Ten percent off at Jenny's Diner. Two lights up on the right, in front of the Marriot. It's a percentage," he said with a wink. "More you spend, more you save."

Back in the room, Stevie had folded up his bed, the baby was babbling, and Janet agreed it would have to be the diner. She restocked the nylon baby bag, placed the baby in her stroller, and off they went.

The sidewalk leading from the Highland Suites led along the building to a side street where they could either go left, back to a small plaza with a Dunkin Donuts and a Supercuts, or right, out to 216. Across the side street was a steep grass embankment that rose up to an adjacent shopping center. They could see the first few tall yellow letters on the façade of the first building, the B-E-S of BEST BUY. They opted to turn right, Rob leading along a narrow channel of grass beside the curb out to 216, where they stopped at the intersection and looked for a sidewalk, but saw none. The traffic was thick and fast-moving, two lanes each way, with a two-foot concrete divider in the middle. They stood for two complete cycles of light changes, and realized that, due to the calibrated green arrows, traffic was continually moving, with, first, all lanes passing through from both sides, and then, once those lanes came to a halt, a steady stream of cars from the turning lanes, leaving no way to cross.

They walked back along the grass strip and crossed over to climb the embankment toward the Best Buy, Janet taking the baby, Rob the stroller, Stevie scampering up on his own, slipping in a bare spot and muddying his pants.

Fearing he'd have to go back to the hotel and change, Stevie stood still, Rob beside him pausing as well. But when Janet said, "Keep going, Mister, it's part of the adventure," Stevie scrambled up the rest of the way, leading the others to a huge parking lot and, thankfully, a sidewalk beginning at the corner of the Best Buy.

The baby back in his stroller, they walked in the breezeless morning sun past Best Buy and Bed Bath and Beyond, following the sidewalk as it turned ninety degrees to the right past a block of smaller stores—a beauty salon, carpet store, Rite Aid. At the next corner, they could either follow the sidewalk around the Rite Aid back to the continuing mass of storefronts—Staples, Dick's, Toys R Us—or cut across the parking lot toward an Outback Steakhouse, which constituted its own island. Beyond the Outback, Rob could see another island, an Applebees, and beyond it a traffic light where he hoped they could cross over to the diner.

"No," Janet said before he could step off the curb. "We're not traipsing as an entire family through a parking lot."

Rob nodded. Janet was right. And besides, this was why they hadn't brought the car in the first place, to get out in the world, take *the long way.*

The plaza and sidewalk ended at the far edge of the Home Depot, a guard rail marking the perimeter of the property, beyond the guard rail a large gas station with convenience store and Subway, beyond that another shopping plaza. Janet raised an arm and pointed toward the highway—actually, Rob noticed, she pointed across it where he saw the Marriot, and before it, the red neon sign atop Jenny's Diner. Having no choice, they turned into the parking lot, walking toward the traffic light.

Rob reached down and mussed Stevie's hair. "Going to Jenny's Diner," he said. "Gonna get us some breakfast!"

"Where is it?" Stevie said.

"Just across the street," Janet said.

"Mama Bear leading the way!" Rob said.

Rob had started calling Janet "Mama Bear" soon after Stevie was born. Although her lifestyle choices were progressive—they belonged to the Bay Street Theater as well as the Nature Conservancy—as a mother she was cautious to the extreme.

Each day before Stevie went out to bike on their cul de sac in North Haven, she'd place obstacles in the road to slow down the occasional motorist, strategically placing unused bicycles, step ladders, whatever conspicuous, portable object she could grab from the storage portion of the garage, leaving just enough room on the street for a car to wriggle past.

One day, alarmed at the speed with which a neighbor had woven through her obstacle course, apparently having grown accustomed to it, she lugged out an old unused easel, planting it beside the tandem bicycle already in place, even making an extra trip to set out a palette of paints on a small table beside the easel.

"This'll get their attention," she said to Rob, standing by.

"Might make them speed up," Rob had quipped, Janet responding with a small groan.

Rob had an anti-artist streak Janet had always attributed to his Reagan-loving father, something Rob wasn't proud of, but which leaked out now and then.

Janet and Rob had an ongoing disagreement as to which of them was more conservative. Rob's family background, along with his job as village bookkeeper, put him at a disadvantage, but each night as they got in bed, he'd recap something Janet had done in an effort to even the score.

Most recently, she'd joined the East End chapter of MATT, Mothers Against Texting Teens, and though Rob agreed driving while texting was a scourge in need of a response, he also sensed in the group more than a bit of sanctimony.

"It's not that I don't admire the intention," Rob had explained to Janet one night as they brushed their teeth side by side, the baby's monitor at one end of the vanity, Stevie's at the other, both turned up to full volume as they ran the water. "What I take issue with is the attitude, as if every accident in the world should be prevented. I mean, we've got our kids living in bubbles, going from helmets to seatbelts to sitting in locked classrooms and houses."

"And the kids addicted to opioids?" Janet said. "How do they fit into this bubble theory?"

"They're so cloistered, they're trying to escape the only way they can," Rob said.

"No," Janet said. "The addicts are the ones most in need of the structure, the support, you're complaining about."

"That's another issue—economic inequality. What I'm talking about is immobilizing people due to fear, *paralyzing* them."

"Maybe it's you that's paralyzed," Janet said with a huff.

Rob shut off the faucet and placed his toothbrush in the rack. This was how most of their arguments ended, with one of them breaking the rule not to levy personal attacks during intellectual disagreements.

"Mama Bear disqualified," he announced, exiting the bathroom, "*ad hominem* attack in the second round."

Seeing the fresh sheets turned back, Rob clapped his hands together, shaking off the disagreement.

"Gonna get me some shut-eye," he said, "and in the morning I'm going to wake up and it's going to be Thursday!"

They meandered through the parking lot which had traffic lanes every couple hundred feet, Rob instructing Stevie to check for back-up lights when walking behind cars.

As they approached the traffic light on 216, Rob had an unobstructed view of Jenny's, beyond it the Marriot, and beyond that, another large hotel coming into view, a Travelodge. Two turning lanes on the far side led toward the hotels, and as they continued walking, Rob saw the road was a thoroughfare, a Walmart and another row of stores becoming visible around the bend beyond the Travelodge.

Recalling the hazy line of mountains he'd seen in the distance from the hotel room, Rob wondered how far the commercial sprawl extended, how far before it turned to countryside.

Coming to the curb at the edge of the parking lot, only a strip of grass, again with no sidewalk, separating them from 216, Rob looked up the highway to the next traffic light, which appeared to be less complicated, though also had neither sidewalk nor crosswalk. He surveyed the restaurants they had passed, the Outback and Applebees, or more precisely the parking lots that encircled them, which were nearly empty. No, they hadn't yet opened.

Together, Rob and Janet lifted the stroller over the tall curb, Stevie latching on as well, and the family stood together on the small grass median watching the unbroken traffic on 216, two lanes moving each way, each side with turning lanes. A few yards to their side, two long lines of cars waited to exit the parking lot, and across the highway, four more lanes, two waiting to release a growing mass of cars, two empty ones waiting to receive the next burst into the Marriot, Travelodge, Walmart and whatever lay beyond.

"Where is everybody going?" Janet shouted above the roar. "We're in the middle of Massachusetts at nine o'clock in the morning!"

"Listen," Rob said, "when this side of 216 gets red lights and a red arrow, we can make it to the divider."

"There's no signal for this lane," Janet said, gesturing at the lane immediately before them turning into the shopping center."

"We'll wait for an opening," Rob said.

"And when we make it to the middle, *if* we make it to the middle," Janet said, "then what do we do?"

Rob gazed across the way, the traffic on 216 momentarily paused as on the far side, the next dam-release of cars shot out onto 216, one lane heading east, the other west. The moment it stopped, the far side of 216 shot into motion, a green arrow directing a lane toward them into the shopping center, and so on, Rob studying each stage of the complex 6-step cycle, not one of them allowing pedestrians to cross.

"The traffic turning onto 216 seems a bit lighter," Rob said, not ready to give up.

He looked down at the baby in the stroller who was asleep, then at Stevie, who, overwhelmed by the noise and rushing traffic, realized it was no time to speak.

"Let's go for it," Rob said to Janet. "We'll make it to the divider and somebody will stop and let us go."

"And if they don't stop?" Janet said. "Then what?"

"We're not asking them to donate a kidney," Rob said, "just to let us cross the street."

"We'd have a better chance getting a kidney," Janet said.

Ever since, a few months after they'd gotten married, they'd seen *Streetcar* at Bay Street, Janet afterward not sympathizing with Blanche's helplessness but excoriating it—"The kindness of strangers?" she'd said, "I can't even rely on the kindness of *friends*!"—Rob had noticed the fierceness of her self-reliance, which since getting married, seemed to be getting stronger. Two years later, when Stevie was born, she seemed to dig in even deeper, and that was when he'd begun calling her Mama Bear.

"So what do you want to do?" Rob asked. "Go back?"

"I want to eat breakfast!" Janet said. "I want my children to eat breakfast!"

Hearing the desperation in Janet's voice, Stevie burst out crying. The baby, lying on her back, stirred awake, saw Rob looming above and gurgled.

Rob removed his cell phone from his pocket. "I'll call a taxi," he said.

"To take us across the street?" Janet said.

"Don't worry," Rob said, scrolling through the search results, "we'll have to walk a mile just to find a place it can pick us up."

"We're not taking a taxi," Janet said.

Again, Rob realized she was right. He wasn't sure why, but knew she was.

"Then the only option is to walk back to the hotel," he said.

"I don't know," Janet said.

Rob stepped closer, keeping Stevie close. "Janet," he said.

"It just seems there ought to be a way," she said.

"There is," he said, as softly as possible given the roar of traffic.

"I can't do it if it doesn't make sense," she said.

"Come on." Rob touched her shoulder. "We'll go back. Hell, by the time we reach the Outback, it'll be open for lunch."

Janet looked at him with dark eyes, weighted with resolution—not the eyes of a mother willing to fight.

"No," she said.

Rob turned and looked up 216, then back the other way, the traffic unabated, if anything growing thicker.

He looked again at his wife of eight years. "Okay," he said.

Janet offered a smile and took Stevie's hand in hers, placing her other one on the handle of the stroller, the baby down there gazing unknowingly out at the world.

Rob's first step was unsure, but once on the highway, he broke into a dash, the loafers not coming loose as he feared but clinging to his feet. He made it to the center and, seeing an opening, hurdled the divider, shot the gap, and bounded safely onto the opposite curb.

Rob stood a moment to pull in a long clearing breath, then turned to see his family across the way, flashing between the six lanes of passing cars, Janet gazing back, not at him, not between the speeding cars but *at* them, her expression stupefied, amazed.

They just keep coming, she thought. *They just keep coming.*

Louse Point

I teach all day downtown, the guy in the subway station with the eye patch and sign and cup there at six a.m. and again at four on my way back, come home to my fifth floor studio with a landline with no voice mail that just rings and rings, turn on the TV and don't watch.

I've just settled on the last ten minutes of House of Cards when out of nowhere my salivary glands start cranking and I am overtaken by this perfectly formed desire for Vienna Fingers. I grab my coat to go down to the Korean market on the corner of ninety-first, only it's just going on six o'clock, right when Babiak comes home from his hot-shit stock broker job, and I can't bear seeing him and asking how his day went and having him shrug and say, "I'm thinking about giving it up and becoming a teacher," and me thinking, Sure you are, but saying "I know what you mean, I've been thinking about making some changes too," and him smiling cause I understand and offering me a beer and me going upstairs to his one bedroom with a balcony and drinking beer out of a glass, then coming back to my studio and heating up leftover French fries and sitting on the couch to watch—or not watch—Monday Night Football, Babiak up there rolling out rice to make goddam sushi—one more person carving out a life for himself in this city teeming with ambition and direction and purpose.

So after I pound down two Coors Lite Tallboys and a carton of mac and cheese, and not-watch some CNN and the first quarter of the game, what do I do? Call up Babiak and ask if he's watching the game. The Browns just scored on a play where the guy stepped out of bounds, and I ask him if the ref blew the call. Babiak's too diplomatic to say, "Hell yeah, botched it big time," instead saying, "Depends what angle of the replay they looked at, because the NFL runs a different tape than ABC." I say, "I guess, though that ref has blown a shitload of calls," and this time Babiak agrees. "Yeah," he says, "if he had one more eye he'd be a Cyclops." And I'm thinking, you didn't have to say that, you don't have to take my side. You on the top floor with your tomorrow of Wall Street and its roaring bull market, me down here in my four-hundred foot studio with 34 spring-loaded fourth-graders, just sitting there at their desks waiting for me.

Next night Babiak knocks on my door and asks if I've got an extra cold one and I say sure, got one shipped straight from the Rockies, and he walks in and sits on the futon without even taking off his goddam Burberry Trench Coat and I'm thinking, another rough day making gobs of money and you need to talk and make it okay, only I start talking first, not to avoid the banality of what he is going to say—what I say is a hundred times dumber than anything he could possibly come up with.

I tell him about my sister, Ronnie, how she calls me up and talks and talks.

Babiak, who met her a few weeks earlier when she came in to the city to pick up a bootlegged TV, wants to know where she's coming from, what time she's getting in.

"Keep it in your knickers," I say, "she's got a kid."

"Oh yeah?" he says, not at all put off. "How old?"

"Like five."

I end up agreeing to call her tomorrow and invite her in. We'll all go to dinner. And I'm already seeing it play out—him losing interest and her not knowing how to read him, calling me up to ask what his not calling really means.

Next day, Ronnie sounds cautious but hopeful—God, I wish she'd be skeptical for once—a twenty-nine year old stock broker that likes kids? But she says she's got nothing planned and comes on in, the three of us going out to eat, Babiak picking up the tab, and afterward she and Babiak go to Stan's for a drink and I head back to my studio.

I'm sitting there not-watching The Late Show when the phone rings and I pick up to hear the voice of Joany, Ronnie's step-daughter—did I mention her? Ronnie's ex-husband is a Denver businessman and when they bought a house out on Louse Point, he moved his daughter from his first marriage, Joany, out to live with Ronnie while he mostly kept traveling, stopping in just long enough to knock up Ronnie. The summer after I quit college, I took the empty guest room that shared a bath with Joany's room and after about three weeks of the most intense attraction I've ever felt for anyone, Joany and I got together. The sex was torturous, both of us starting and stopping, starting and stopping. I'd never had a long term relationship and Joany had moved around all her life, each relationship she'd had getting cut short by her father's next move—we were a perfect match.

In the fall I took a job driving the van for the food pantry and picked her up each day after she got off work as a mother's helper.

I don't know if it was immoral or not, and I don't know if we were in love or locked in some kind of blind need, but anybody who claims to know the difference is full of shit anyway.

What I do know is that if it hurt Ronnie, she didn't show it; in fact, she seemed to like us being together, as if it felt good to have the different threads of her life finally connecting. Like now, if her jet-setting husband ever dumped her, or *when* he dumped her, and took Joany away, she'd have, through me, a connection from a different angle, another way to hold on. She even let Joany and me move into the master bedroom, only clearing us out every couple of months when the husband came to town, and as her belly grew rounder with the child, she cooked our meals and washed our clothes.

Then one day I came in to find Ronnie, eight months pregnant, doubled over her sewing machine. A pair of my torn work jeans were placed in the machine and I didn't even need to ask what was wrong.

The hell of it was, my moving out didn't help. I mean it helped me and Ronnie, and it also helped me and Joany begin the inevitable long, drawn out break-up, which would take over a year, but it didn't bring the husband around any more frequently, and they were divorced about the same time Joany and I finally called it quits.

I remember Ronnie the weekend it finally came through—he was in Tobago or someplace and his lawyer had been sending copy after copy of the papers to be signed, Ronnie ignoring them, till finally one day this Fed Ex chick showed up and she and Ronnie started talking and they had a couple mutual friends, and Fed Ex was a hot shit surfer and Ronnie had always wanted to surf. This chick tells her she's got an extra board, no problem, just come out to Ditch Saturday morning, and Ronnie, while they're talking, just opens the envelope, signs about five papers, seals them in the Express Return, hands it back to Fed Ex. "What the hell," she said to me, walking back in the house, "I always wanted to surf."

That night we had a sit-down dinner and she was gay as hell, the baby crawling around between our legs, and me and her and Joany had a glass of wine and then, when Ronnie served us dinner, I saw it.

Now that my dick was finally down, I saw they weren't my pants in that sewing machine that day, it wasn't me she was serving the plate of cous cous and lamb strips to, it wasn't even me who'd Joany'd grabbed onto like her life depended on it. Sitting at that table between the husbandless wife and the fatherless teenager wasn't me at all.

So it's about midnight and Babiak and Ronnie must be on their fourth or fifth drink, or maybe switched over to wine by now, and Joany tells me she's just returned to Denver—she has graduated college and taken a job in her father's business, and she says she's working on her MBA at night and she just wanted to call to thank me for helping her through a really tough period. Not sure how two years of sputtering toward a dead-end could have helped anybody, I tell her not to mention it.

But the sweetness in her voice gets to me, sitting there on Friday night not watching Jay Leno, Ronnie and Babiak out there sipping wine, maybe even dancing by now, perhaps exchanging their first kiss. Sweetness and a faint note of longing—as if maybe it wasn't as worthless as I make it out to be.

So what do I say, completely and absolutely filled with the knowledge that she not only won't but can't? "Maybe you should come back to New York." Instantly, I hear how the words once spoken chase away the wisp of possibility, take that little sliver of dream and kill it cold.

Still, it's like, what the fuck, you got to at some point ask for *something.*

Joany says what she must: "This *is* back, Ricky. I've already gone back." And I feel this surge of emotion for her, for escaping, for being safe and whole, out there in the world.

I wish Ronnie and Babiak luck tonight, I really do. For God's sake she's my sister, and Babiak, he's my neighbor, my friend, and though I know his fondness for her kid will wear off after a few evenings of her not being available, I also know that tonight the kid is home with a sitter and the two of them are clinking drinks at Stan's with its low hanging chandeliers that throw just barely enough light to see.

And next week or the week after, when Babiak stops in for a beer, sits down on my futon in his coat and hat and says nice things about Ronnie in that deathly summing up tone, I will only half listen as he continues, saying how kind she is, what a great job she's doing raising that kid by herself. And a few days later Ronnie will call and say how considerate and supportive he is, not really the stock broker type at all, only he hasn't called her and she's not sure what to make of it. I'll tell her not to worry about it, that it's working itself out for the best, that he's probably more complicated than he makes himself out to be, and she'll ask me if I think she should call him. I'll say no, but she'll persist, and I'll hear that slim, faint glimmer of hope in her voice—that blind, stupid, utterly unjustifiable hope—and I'll pull in a deep breath, slowly release it, and say, "Sure, give him a call. What do you have to lose?"

Wiborg

When Michael returned home from an afternoon surfing crisp autumn waves at Wiborg, he found an envelope taped to the door containing a letter from Vivvy, who'd moved out a month earlier to stay with a friend.

This letter is simply to clarify a couple of things. I only said you never loved me because I was hurt. I do not blame you.

> Next, I realize I have not been a good mother for Tommy. I have talked with her about this, but the last thing a fifteen year old needs is a mother making things worse.
>
> I left a box of things for her in my room at Dorothy's. I am not acting out of pain. On the contrary, I am seeing things more clearly than ever. You hear me, Michael? Let me do this.
>
> Genevieve

Michael grabbed his shaving bag from the bathroom and a roll of cash from the top drawer of his bedroom dresser.

When he reached the door to the garage, Tommy entered the house through the front, and Michael turned back as she walked into the kitchen.

"Why aren't you at the Harvest Fair?" Michael said.

"My ride had to leave. What happened?"

"I think your mother left town. I need to track her down."

"Where?"

"Probably the house in Connecticut."

"I'm going with you."

"You can't, Tommy."

"I have to," Tommy said.

Michael stared at her a moment. "Okay," he said, "get in the truck."

The two of them drove in silence up the Long Island Expressway, Michael calling Vivvy's cell every twenty minutes, crossed the Throgs Neck Bridge, and forked onto the parkway into Connecticut.

"What did she say?" Tommy asked finally.

Michael released a deep breath. "She said this is because of her, not you."

"What is?"

"Her not being there for you."

"If she's not there for me, how does leaving help?"

Michael cruised along in the passing lane, winding up the parkway into Litchfield County, where Vivvy had grown up with her grandmother, in a small cottage beside a preserve.

Pulling into the driveway, they saw Vivvy's car.

"Wait here," Michael said.

He entered the kitchen, calling Vivvy's name, then walked upstairs. Finding both bedrooms empty, he looked out a window into the back yard and saw her. She stood at the edge of the lawn where the mowed green grass met the tall yellow grass of the neighboring field. Michael walked downstairs and out the back door, slowing as he approached.

Vivvy turned back with a wan smile.

"Hold on," Michael said, and he jogged back to the side of the house and called to Tommy, "We're in the back!"

Tommy came around the corner of the house and, reaching them, gripped the front of Vivvy's sweater and pressed her face into Vivvy's neck.

"I'm happy to see you," Vivvy said. "I'm always happy to see you."

Vivvy stepped away from them, reached down and snapped a piece of long grass from the neighboring field, then turned back, her eyes filling. "That's why I have to step away," she said. "So I can see you."

The three of them spent the night upstairs, Tommy sharing with Vivvy the room with two twin beds, Michael in the room next door, and in the morning, sat together on the back patio drinking tea. Michael suggested Vivvy begin reducing her medication, and Vivvy said she'd stopped it a couple of months ago, and Michael said then maybe she needed to get back on it.

"If I'm going to do this," Vivvy said, "it has to be on my own."

"Do what?" Tommy said.

"Make a life," Vivvy said.

Michael made eggs, and Tommy brought the plates out to the patio, and afterward they played cards, the breeze blowing Vivvy's hair into her face, Michael watching her push it back behind her ear, exchanging a hopeful look with Tommy, and in the evening Michael went out and returned with deli salads and sandwiches which Vivvy barely touched.

The second day was again sunny and warm for October and the three of them moved in and out through the sliding doors to the patio, Vivvy sitting for a while in the sun, going in for a nap.

In the late afternoon, Vivvy said she was hungry and Michael went to the market. When he returned, Vivvy and Tommy were in the living room watching a documentary on the National Parks, and Michael set the food on the coffee table.

"We visited Grand Teton and Yellowstone when your mother was pregnant with you," Michael said to Tommy. "Your mother insisted she needed to go hiking."

"And Mr. Surfer Boy could barely keep up with me," Vivvy said.

"How far along were you, Viv," Michael said, "five months?"

"Seven," Vivvy said, turning to Tommy. "You were starting to kick up a storm, and I was like, if I just sit around this girl's going to beat the hell out of me."

"I still don't get why you named me Tommy."

"It is *not* a boy's name," Michael said.

"And even if it is," Vivvy said, "your father's Uncle Tommy was amazing."

"I also knew a girl in college named Tommy," Michael said.

"Don't complain," Vivvy said, "I was named after my grandmother, Maman Genevieve, who made me, as a child, take a salt bath every night and dunk my head under."

"That explains a lot," Tommy said, glancing at Michael.

"She is rather salty," Michael said.

"Come here," Vivvy said. She opened her arms, and Tommy stepped over and buried her face against Vivvy's shoulder.

The next morning, they locked up the house and Tommy rode with Vivvy, Michael leading for a while, then following, as they slid down from New England, crossing the bridge onto the island and heading east.

As he trailed along through the Pine Barrens and past the few remaining potato fields, he lost sight of them, drove hard for a while to catch up, then relaxed. Now that they were back on the East End, there was really only one way to go.

A few days later, Vivvy called Michael to say Dorothy had offered to let Vivvy share the lease, but she thought she needed her own place.

"There's an apartment I saw," Vivvy said.

When Vivvy had moved out, Michael had agreed it would be best for her to do it on her own. But now it was no longer a question of helping her leave, but helping her stay—the perimeter had just broadened a bit.

"I can cover the deposit," Michael said. "Whatever it takes to get you in."

"Thank you," Vivvy said.

"Listen," Michael said, "Tommy and I are heading over to Wiborg for a walk. Can you meet us?"

"I can meet you," Vivvy said.

Michael and Tommy pulled up to the beach and saw Vivvy standing at the water's edge, wrapped in a coat, facing into the wind off the ocean.

As they approached, Vivvy turned back. "I don't love it out here," she said.

"Why?" Tommy said, and Vivvy smiled and looked back at the sea.

"Having the ocean right here in your back yard …" Michael said.

"Every fall is like a funeral," Vivvy said.

"It's that way everywhere in the fall," Michael said.

"No," Vivvy said, glancing at Tommy. "Here, when all the people leave, it's just water and emptiness."

"When we were kids," Michael said, "on Labor Day we'd stand in town and wave at the line of cars, their stuff all piled on their roofs, driving back to the city, and the next day was so quiet. Tumbleweed Tuesday."

"The place I found is in Mattituck," Vivvy said. "Cheaper than here, less seasonal."

"Are you moving?" Tommy asked.

"I'm going to see you as much as I do now," Vivvy said. "It's only forty minutes away."

"Do you have to?" Tommy said, and she stepped close beside Vivvy who continued gazing at the ocean.

"It's hard to let go," Vivvy said softly, "but necessary."

"Mommy," Tommy said.

Vivvy turned to her. "I mean hard to let go of East Hampton," she said. She smiled and took Tommy in her arms, the two the same height. "I won't ever let go of you."

Michael and Tommy tossed some stones into the breakers, and the three of them strolled up the beach.

"I have no problem with coming back," Vivvy said. "Once I get free of this place, I may start enjoying it again. You know," she said, "stepping away to see things better."

"And Daddy and I will go to Mattituck," Tommy said.

"Absolutely," Michael said.

They walked past the Maidstone Clubhouse, the pool beside it covered for the winter, then turned back.

When they returned to Wiborg, Tommy stopped. "Come here," she said, and facing the ocean, she pulled Michael to one side, linking her arm in his, and pulled Vivvy close to her other side.

Tommy clung to each of their arms, gazing straight out to sea, grimacing into the wind.

"Smile," she said, "God is taking our picture."

PROMISED LAND

"He won't let me do anything," Melanie said. "Either I travel with him as his personal servant or sit home and wait for him to get back."

For the past three nights, Danny had sat with his sister on the deck facing the bay, the warm July breeze and steady wash of the waves easing her into a calm from which she could speak, yet also making her complaints seem, by contrast, temperamental, excessive.

"I know he loves me," she said. "But it's not right, and it's worse for Lorena, who, by the way, I'm getting to hate."

Since marrying Eduardo eight months earlier, Melanie had had had sporadic success mothering Lorena, his nine year old from an earlier marriage.

"You've got a villa in Mexico," Danny said, "an apartment in Paris, this beach house. Things could be a lot worse, Melanie."

Her eyes left the bay and, glinting in the light from the moon that had risen behind them, found his. She forced a smile. "You'll see," she said. "If you think I've been living it up, you'll see."

~

After three years of travelling, sometimes with Melanie, sometimes without, Eduardo had finally delivered on his promise for a vacation back at the house he'd bought years earlier in the area of Napeague called Promised Land, just a few miles from where Melanie and Danny had grown up in Amagansett. Danny had come out to join them for a short vacation from upstate where he was working as a carpenter's assistant and trying to finish college.

"He said he wants to take you on a dig in Mexico," Melanie said.

Eduardo had been an archaeology professor in Guadalajara but had branched off into dealing pre-Columbian art.

"I'm not holding my breath," Danny said.

"Tell me about it," Melanie said. Then she raised her eyes to the sky, mottled with clouds, and shook her head. "At least we're both back home."

"Why not move back for good?" Danny asked.

"Because I can *do* things here." She turned in her seat and faced him, mimicking Eduardo's deep voice: "This Long Island is no place for a woman."

Hearing a distant drumming that gradually grew louder, the two sat in silence and watched two horses run past on the beach before them. The same two horses, their muscles rounded in shadow, had run by each of the last three nights, increasingly visible as the moon had grown.

The door opened and Lorena's small brown head appeared. She had to have it shaved because of lice. In the dark, she looked like a tiny old man.

"Melanie," she said in English, the language of her Mexican school for Internationals, "can I have some ice cream?"

"Yes, Sweety."

The door closed quietly and Melanie said, "I really do love her. We're just always being pulled in different directions."

The door again swung open, and this time Eduardo stepped onto the porch. He wore leather pants cinched tight with a drawstring and a loose white shirt that shone beneath his dark brown face.

"Did she ask you, Melanie, for the ice cream?" he said.

"Yes," she groaned.

"Why you talking to me like this?"

Melanie didn't respond.

"If there is something wrong, you tell me and not talk like a child."

Danny stared across the bay to the dark shoreline of Amagansett. Where the blackness of the sand cliffs met the grey of the sky ran a faint yellow stream of light.

Eduardo knelt beside Melanie and turned her face toward him with a finger. "You have been crying," he said.

"Allergies," she said.

Eduardo looked at Danny. "She loves to cry, this one. She think she must keep the bay full when it does not rain."

Eduardo stood. "We going to have ice cream now," he said, and stepped back through the door.

Again they heard the rumbling of the returning horses and through the soft light of the moon, the dark bodies passed back before them. Danny and Melanie watched until the rumbling had faded and it was again still, with only a gentle flicker of moonlight on the bay.

"Has he said anything to you about his next trip?" Melanie asked.

"Taking me on a dig is the last thing on his mind."

"You never know," she said whimsically.

"I'm can't just hang out waiting. I've got to get back to work."

Melanie pointed to a toad on the edge of the porch, casting a shadow clear enough for them to see its pulsing throat. When Danny spoke, the toad hopped into the grass.

"What about you?" he said. "Going back to Mexico?"

"Who can say what I'll do?"

"Melanie, you've got to say."

"I know," she said, repeating in a drone, "I know, I know, I know."

They sat a moment in silence, then Melanie rose slowly from her chair. "Come on," she said, "he wants us to have ice cream."

"I'll pass," Danny said.

Danny sat alone in the last of the dying breeze, a cloud moving in front of the moon, its edges glowing. Then it shoved past and the dark bay again became visible, the path of moonlight no longer dappled but, due to the stillness, arranged in languid ovals.

Eduardo came out on the porch and sat next to Danny with a bottle and a shot glass. He poured one and swallowed it, then looked at Danny. "Here, I pour one for you. Just one, more than that is no good."

Danny drank it. The unfamiliar liquor was sweet but strong.

"I am seeing," Eduardo began, his leathery hands tapping the arms of his chair, "this place is no good for a woman."

Danny met Eduardo's dark shimmering eyes.

"She can't live like this," Eduardo continued. "She need a home. At the same time she doesn't want what she have and she afraid she going to lose it."

"I think she wants to stay here," Danny said.

"No," Eduardo said. "She always wanting to run. She have to learn to be a wife now. She cannot go home and be a daughter, a sister. No more of this running." He paused, then added, "I get her a house in Mexico and maybe I go back to the university, where she can do cooking and gardening and all these things. Otherwise," he smiled at Danny, "she keep filling the bay and not letting the rain."

A toad again appeared on the deck, a few feet before Eduardo. He leaned forward and sprung his hand at it, but it leapt away. "In Mexico I catch lizards," he said and grinned. "One with each hand."

"It'll be a while before you go back to the university," Danny said. "In the meantime, why not let her live here?"

"No, here Melanie go crazy. She think I keep her from the world. The truth is I *protect* her from the world."

"She doesn't need to be protected," Danny began, but before he could continue Eduardo lifted a hand and raised his chin, listening. Danny heard the distant thundering of the horses.

Eduardo stood. "Come," he said, leading Danny into the sand as the pounding grew louder.

One head became visible bobbing above the black curving shore behind. Then the other, smaller head bobbed into the charcoal sky.

As they approached, Eduardo emitted a low "Wo," then again, "W-o-o," and the horses, mother and colt, slowed to a stop as they saw the two men. Eduardo continued the sound as he approached the stepped carefully toward the mother, the colt close at her side.

Eduardo touched the mare's neck, then massaged it with his fingers. "Listen to me," he said. He grabbed a handful of her mane. "Listen to me now."

The colt shifted nervously, but the mother held firm.

Eduardo turned to the colt. "What's the matter with you?" He reached out to it and it jumped back, triggering the mother to dance back, whinny, and rear, holding her forelegs in the air above Eduardo, before swinging around on her hind legs and running off, the colt tight on her flank as they disappeared into the dark.

Danny stepped forward from where he had retreated. "Mom got a little upset," he said.

"She just making a fuss. Because she feel my control, like a—" Eduardo searched for the word—"like a harness."

"I don't know," Danny said. 'When you reached for her colt—"

"I do know," Eduardo said. "I'm not asking 'Can I touch your colt?' so she have nothing to say."

They walked back to the house. Danny was unconvinced; it was only goodness that had kept that horse from crashing down on Eduardo with her hooves, some instinctive benevolence, that led her away from conflict rather than toward it.

They reached the porch and found Melanie standing in the doorway. "Are you coming to bed now?" she said to Eduardo.

"Yes, Sweety. Look at those eyes," he said to Danny. "*Mas lagrimas que anos*. More tears than years. I like the English."

"Danny," Melanie said, "I'll see you in the morning and cook us all a nice breakfast. You'll be glad you came, I promise."

"Okay," Danny said.

Melanie walked back inside and Danny stepped forward, looked into Eduardo's dark face. "She's better off living here," he said.

Eduardo took a step back. "Your sister is confused, but she is a good person. She stay with me, and I get her a house in Guadalajara. Because she is good."

"You mean she's afraid. Afraid to leave you."

"No. You drink water because it is good, not because you afraid of dying." He laughed lightly. "She need me, and I need her. You people afraid of that word."

Eduardo walked three paces to the railing, bent low, and took a sudden swipe at a toad, nearly grabbing it, but instead knocking it reeling into the sand. "*Puta*." He turned back to Danny. "All this wanting, that is her problem. She want to be a daughter and a wife; she want to feel the sand on her feet and the moon in her hand."

"But she does *not* want to go back to Mexico."

Eduardo shook his head. "It is not about wanting but about doing. These wants she have are just these feelings." He fluttered his fingers in the air. "You can always want something different—you can always think something different—but it's what you do."

Danny was quiet, thinking yes it's true, Melanie has always wanted more than what she has. At the same time, he recalled the late-night phone calls from Mexico City, thought of little Lorena exiled to boarding school in Cuernevaca, and felt Eduardo's explanation was too easy.

Eduardo put a hand on Danny's shoulder. "Don't kill yourself thinking. You still a young man. Tomorrow we go fishing, out deep, and you get something. Something to put your hands on."

"I'm thinking about leaving tomorrow," Danny said.

Eduardo chuckled. "As long as you only thinking about it," he said. "First we go fishing. We get you a nice fish."

Danny looked at Eduardo's smiling face, any difference in opinion erased, the thought of reeling in a swordfish or marlin trilling his stomach. If he couldn't go on an expedition, he could go deep-sea fishing. Yet something was too easy.

"We'll bring Melanie," Danny said.

Eduardo didn't answer but stared over Danny's shoulder to the beach. Danny waited for a response, then turned to see what Eduardo was looking at.

The horses were standing on the beach, mother motionless, colt at its side anxiously shuffling its feet. They stood facing the house, their sides facing the moon layered in shadows, with phosphorescent streaks where their fur glinted against the dark backdrop of water.

"Okay," Eduardo said, "go get your sister."

Danny waited for an explanation then, not getting one, went to the back bedroom and found Melanie in her white nightgown changing the sheets.

"Eduardo wants you outside."

"It's okay," she said, "You guys go ahead and talk."

"The horses are there."

She looked up from the sheets. "What's he doing?"

"I'm not sure."

Melanie started for the door. "What's he doing to those horses?" she said, and Danny followed her to the porch where he saw Eduardo by the water with the horses, silhouetted against the bay, and followed Melanie down into the sand.

The mare held still as Eduardo rubbed her head. Continuing to stroke her, he circled, for a moment separating her from the colt, and she stamped her feet.

"You a wonderful woman," he said. "You a wonderful proud woman."

"What's he doing?" Melanie whispered to Danny.

"*He* is going to show you something," Eduardo said, stepping in front of the mare and peering into her eyes. "Now I ride on you," he told her.

"Eduardo, stop it," Melanie said.

Eduardo moved to the mare's side, massaging and pressing down on her back, readying it for the weight, then turned to Melanie. "She is a riding horse. From the farm by the highway."

The horse snorted, as if impatient with the talk.

"Okay, okay," Eduardo said.

He swung his body onto her back and she immediately reared, sending him sliding off the other side. Landing on his feet, Eduardo laughed from deep in his stomach.

"Yes, you some woman," he said. "You want me to work. Okay, this time I ride."

Eduardo jumped up and stayed on, the horse kicking, but not as hard, and spinning in a half circle.

"Woman, easy," he said.

"She doesn't want to do this," Melanie said.

Eduardo didn't answer her but spoke to the horse. "Now we go. Hyah, hyah."

He snapped his heels into her belly, and the mare snorted, releasing a high whinny through flapping lips, and leaped into a gallop. The colt followed close behind.

In a few minutes they returned, and Eduardo slid off the side opposite the colt, holding his hand against the horse's panting body.

"Now, Melanie," Eduardo said, "you ride."

"*What?*" she said.

"Yes. You ride now. Your brother says you can't wait anymore. You need to go fish with me, or you need to be home again. You have all these ideas. So you ride this horse." His lips trembled as his voice rose. "You do what I do."

"What are you talking about?" she said. "You were crazy to begin with, riding that horse." She looked from Eduardo to Danny. "What's going on out here?"

"Eduardo—" Danny said.

"Yes," Eduardo continued, "you supposed to be there, in one place. But you keep dreaming, you keep running away in your mind. Now you run, right here."

"This is what you guys have been talking about all this time," she said, "how to get me on some horse in the middle of the night?"

"No, Melanie," Danny said.

"Okay then," she said, still looking at Danny. "I'll ride the damned horse. And maybe I won't come back. Or maybe this thing will just go ahead and kill me." She moved toward the horse and it neighed loudly, flailing its mane.

"It's okay," Eduardo coaxed, his voice now gentle. "She just making a fuss."

"Just like the old days," Danny offered. "Cedar Farm."

Melanie moved mechanically to the horse's side and, with a lift from Eduardo, swung onto it and gazed back at the two men. The horse and colt stood motionless.

Melanie reached to the base of the neck with both hands as Eduardo had done, feeling for something to hold on to, and as her hands gripped the horse's flesh it leaped forward into a gallop, the colt following.

As they disappeared into the darkness, Danny turned to Eduardo. "You don't know my sister," he said, but Eduardo didn't answer, just stared ahead into the night.

A large cloud had moved in front of the moon, the cloud black in the center but lightening to grey, then to glowing white at the edges. The cloud shoved past and across the bay from Promised Land, the sand cliffs sat in an unimpeded half-light, beneath a curtain of black sky. A faint breeze wafted in from the direction the horses had run.

"Come," Eduardo said with a wave of his hand, and began walking up the beach.

Danny looked ahead but could see nothing but the faint outline of water and shore. "Won't she come back?" he asked.

"No," Eduardo said, striding ahead.

Following, Danny peered ahead but still saw nothing, and they followed the horses' deep hoof prints filled with shadow.

Eduardo pointed ahead. Danny looked along the shore and could make out the outlines of the two horses standing by the water.

"Where's Melanie?" Danny said.

“She here.”

He looked again as he caught up with Eduardo and saw they had almost reached her. Melanie sat hunched in the sand, head bowed. Eduardo reached her first and Danny lagged behind, gazing at their shadows on the sand, Eduardo’s and hers. Waiting for them to speak, Danny watched the shapes as a thin line extended from Eduardo’s to hers, and when he lifted his eyes he saw Eduardo’s hand resting on her head, Melanie gazing up at him, her face apologetic, sickly.

“It’s broken,” she said.

“What is, Sweety?” Eduardo said. “The horse? Hah, you broke the horse.”

“My arm,” she said softly.

“No, Sweety. Let me see your arm.”

Eduardo bent forward, took hold and lifted her wrist, and Melanie’s cry cut into the night. He let go, and she rocked her head back, letting the dull light of the moon show her arm. It was disfigured in the forearm, bone pushing the skin out in a point like a second elbow.

Danny stepped over and clutched her shoulder.

“I’m okay,” she said calmly.

“Let’s get her somewhere,” Danny said.

Eduardo stood still, staring at the two of them. “You see?” he said. “You see what happens?” Danny stood up and Eduardo stepped in front of him. “You see now?”

“Not now, Eduardo,” Melanie said.

“See what?” Danny said to him. “That she shouldn’t have ridden the horse?”

“No,” Eduardo said. “That these dreams, these dreams—”

“Please stop talking,” Melanie said.

Eduardo turned to Melanie and bent down before her. "My beauty," he said. "My beauty. You see now?" he said softly, leaning forward, pushing a kiss against her face, then another. "Yes, you do," he said, "you do," and he cupped his hand around her head and pushed his lips against hers.

Melanie twisted her face away, gasping for air. "Eduardo!"

"Yes," Eduardo said, staring into her face. "Yes." Then he lifted her in his arms. "Yes," he repeated, "yes," and began walking up the beach.

Danny followed at a couple of paces, watching Melanie hanging quietly in Eduardo's arms, his head arched over hers, holding a steady gaze into her eyes.

"Danny," Melanie called back, "my bracelet came off."

Danny jogged back to where they had found her. He sifted the sand through his fingers, looking back at their single figure moving up the shore, Melanie's hair catching the moonlight as it swung from Eduardo's arm. Then Danny heard the hooves. He glanced up the beach toward the rumbling, then back at Eduardo and Melanie. Danny moved back and crouched low.

The horses stampeded past him, the colt scarcely keeping the pace. Danny looked ahead of the horses as the gap closed, anticipating Eduardo's response. But Eduardo didn't turn. The horses drew closer, but Eduardo and Melanie, their gazes locked into one another's, didn't seem to hear.

"Melanie!" Danny called, and again, "Melanie!"

Eduardo swung around, and as he faced the horses his arms went slack and Melanie slid to the ground, twisting to land on her feet. She tried to pull him with her good arm out of the way, but couldn't, Eduardo standing there transfixed, gazing drunkenly at the oncoming horses.

As the horses reached them, Melanie pulled herself in to him, burying her face in his chest, and Eduardo doubled his head over hers, averting his eyes from the lead horse, the mother, and together they cringed.

The horses narrowly missed them—later Melanie would claim the mare brushed against her, though Eduardo would insist it was only the wind, horses don't do such things—then, after passing, mother and colt continued up the beach in a fierce gallop, perfectly content to pound the beach.

Camp Hero

In a field
I am the absence of field.
Wherever I am
I am what is missing.
—Mark Strand

Lance

Each day after basketball practice I'd drop Higgins and my cousin Sonny in Freetown, then instead of going home go driving, usually in a long loop, through Springs along the bay and out to Napeague where sometimes I'd turn onto the Highway and cruise out to Montauk Point. By the time I got back to Freetown my mother'd be in bed and my sister, Joany, who hadn't spoken since my father died—he'd been gone for ten years before that—would be lying in her nightly trance before the television.

At Montauk's where I saw Ricky, playing by himself on this secluded black-top basketball court overlooking the ocean in Camp Hero, the deserted WW II army base. First I watched from a distance, him running the court, up and back, up and back, the ball bouncing at his side like it was on a string. He had better game than any white boy on the East End, quite possibly better than any brother. But what did it matter to him, out there playing by his lonesome, taking a game meant to be played with other people, against other people, and turning it into something he couldn't ever lose?

So one day I got out of my car and walked through that cold wind off the ocean over to the court. He just kept shooting, paying me no mind, so I had to ask could I play, and he checks his phone like he's on a tight schedule living out there at the tip of the island all by himself. You could see the roof of his house from the court, a shingled cottage tucked into the trees before the cliffs, the only inhabited building in the camp. One game, I tell him, and though he agreed to play, he never did, not really, and I took the game without even breaking a sweat.

A week later I came back and it was the same thing, him just rolling over, this time two games in a row. So I told him, "Fuck it then, play by yourself," and walked out the gate, not stopping till I heard the chain-link fence rattle behind me. I turned back and he was hanging onto it, peering over at me, behind him only ocean and sky.

"Then why come all the way out here?" he said. "If you're looking to run ball, why come out here?"

"Just looking for a game," I said, and got in my car and left.

Ricky

All fall, I never saw a single soul out there other than two guys from the town who came out once every few weeks to tend the grounds, until one day Lance Williams, star of the high school basketball team, shows up. Must've been November, 'cause when I turned around he was standing there in the gate blowing in his hands.

"Play a game?" he says.

So what do I say, him standing there already on the court, and just like that he's taking out the ball telling me game's to eleven, win by two, and though I hit a couple of shots, the truth was it made absolutely no difference to me if I won or lost. I was only playing because he asked me to.

So he hits a couple, taking the lead, only once he gets the edge he doesn't let up but plays harder, hitting another, and another, running off seven, eight shots in a row, his surest shot of all the one to win it.

Same thing when he came back. The breeze off the ocean was cold and steady, and when I get to the court, there's Lance sitting on the hood of his car. So he beats me again, then insists we play another, and this time kills me.

"You just roll over," he said, grabbing his sweatshirt from the black-top and walking through the gate.

I followed as far as the fence. "Then what're you coming out here for?" I said.

Lance slowly turned around. "Not for this," he said.

Lance

Basketball basketball basketball. We sit in class all day thinking about it, then practice for two hours or maybe have a game, and drive home talking shit about who busted who, and I drop 'em both, Higgins and Sonny, in a fucking trailer park. And though my father's life insurance got us a house—split level ranch in the center of Freetown—the place was too big for us to heat, half the rooms sealed closed with plastic. Every day same as the one before, until Coach comes up to me after practice and asks if everything's okay and I say Sure, why wouldn't it be? and he says, You're not playing like yourself, keep it up and you won't get a scholarship, and I shrug my shoulders, thinking, Fuck a scholarship, and take Higgins and Sonny home to the trailer park and go driving.

It's another of those cold gray east-end days when I pull up to the first beach, Maidstone, only half mile or so from home, and see this figure standing out at the end of the jetty that sticks into the harbor, wearing this purple hat and scarf. On days like that everything blurs into gray—water, land, sky—except now there's these two soft spots of color. Then the figure holds its hands out to the side and turns slowly in a circle, and I realize it's Joany. She spins again and I can barely make out her mouth is moving. I roll down my window but the wind is whipping in off the water too loud to hear anything, yet I see the headphones poking out beneath her hat and her mouth opening and closing like she's singing. Hasn't said a word to anybody in almost a year and she's standing out there in the wind singing.

I continued on around the bay, stopping at Louse Point and Barnes Hole, not seeing a single other person out of doors until I got to Montauk Point and turned into Camp Hero, driving across that open field above the ocean where I saw Ricky shooting hoops.

He hems and haws like usual, talking 'bout how cold it is, but once I challenge him he can't ever say no, and good as he was, even half-assing it I knew he was due to be giving me some trouble—despite himself—and the first two games were tight till the end, then the third was tied at point game, and we went back and forth, neither of us able to score, till finally I said fuck it, sent my forearm into his chest, and dropped in the winner.

Ricky didn't call a foul, just slumped down against the fence, his sweat-soaked t-shirt steaming in the cold air.

"Damn right you're tired," I said. "You actually started playing."

"But not you," he said, "cause you're one hundred percent pure killer, right? I don't know how to win and you don't know how to lose."

I just stood there looking down at him. "I know plenty about losing," I said.

Thanksgiving day my mother cooked a turkey like always for me and Joany, Sonny and his mother, and my father's brother, Uncle Ken. Why the hell she stayed in touch with him, let alone cooked him Thanksgiving dinner, my dad not one or even two steps removed but three, the first step, Joany and me not even old enough for school, he goes to prison for manslaughter (punched some white dude in an adult hoop league, the guy had an epileptic seizure and died), the second, not answering anybody's letters, and the third, getting out and dying in California with us never knowing till three months later.

Still, in they all came, Uncle Ken hugging and kissing everyone, dropping a bottle of eight dollar wine on the table, and turning on the football, my mother setting out drinks and food. Joany sitting there in headphones reading a magazine while my mother tells 'em all how Joany's gonna go to art school, and about the letter I got from Coastal, calling it an offer what wasn't nothing but a form letter sent to prospects, and my Uncle Ken nodding real earnest, saying "I understand Coastal has outstanding academics," like he knows anything at all about the place other than it's near a coast.

So I ate quick and left, driving the loop along the bay and on to Montauk, and sure enough, there's Ricky running the court under that gray sky, just gliding from one end to the other.

"You eat yet?" I said, coming through the gate.

"Eat?" he said.

"Turkey," I said. "You know, the Pilgrims, Plymouth, stealing all that land from the Indians?"

"Nah," he said, "I'll get something later."

"Who all's in there anyway?" I asked, looking toward his house.

"My old man's got a restaurant in the city," he said. "Comes out on Tuesdays. Most of 'em anyway."

"Well," I said, "we got a place for you over at my house. But you have to be quick cause I got some hungry kinfolk."

"Nah," Ricky said, "let's you and me run some ball."

"Well, look at you," I said, and a minute later he's tossing in these bombs, one after another, the game over before I even scored.

"What the fuck you eat for breakfast?" I said.

"Nothing," he said, and we played again, him picking up where he left off, shooting these rainbows from out where there wasn't even no sense guarding him. Then it starts snowing these big wet flakes that melted away as they hit the black-top, but even with the wet ball Ricky kept firing away, spinning around shooting fadeaways, jumpers from the corner falling out of bounds, ball not even hitting the rim, just snapping that rusted metal chain.

After losing three in a row I held up both hands in surrender. "My ass is one hundred percent kicked," I told him and headed for the car. When I looked back, I saw Ricky standing there holding the ball on his hip, watching me, snow flakes collecting on his head and shoulders.

"Come on over and get some food," I said.

"Nah," Ricky said, "snow'll let up soon."

"Get in the car," I told him. "I want you to meet somebody."

Ricky

By the time we got to Freetown Thanksgiving day, the snow had stopped and it was getting dark. We found the house with no lights on, just a dull grey glow in the living room, and Lance took me in to meet his sister, Joany, who was lying on the rug, pillows wedged under her chin. Lance asked her if the others had left and she nodded, and he asked where their mother was and she tipped her head toward the stairs.

Lance got a couple of beers and we sat in the two wooden chairs to Joany's side, only chairs in the room.

"This boy gave me a serious schooling today," Lance said, but Joany's attention didn't leave the set.

"Well," Lance said, chugging the last of his beer and lifting himself to his feet, "there ought to be a ton of leftovers in there. You okay helping yourself?"

I nodded and he carried himself over to the stairs where he looked back at me, lifted his hands over his forehead and flicked his wrist, shooting a ball.

"Gonna get you next time," he said.

Lance smiled, shook his head, and went up the stairs.

The last time I'd been alone with a girl was in fifth grade when Cindy Karlo came over after school and played board games. My mother had moved out a few weeks before and I got this idea it was time to start dating. It was like a reflex, I had to date someone, but forcing it didn't work, just pushed the girls farther away, so I backed off.

In ninth grade my father moved me from the city out to Camp Hero where my mother, who'd been denied custody, couldn't keep showing up unexpected (I was supposed to spend every other weekend with her in the city), and where the school, East Hampton High, twenty miles away, was supposedly better. Never occurred to my father I'd have to bike two miles just to get the bus.

Now here I am sitting in this half-dark room with Lance's sister lying there on her stomach, the only light the dim glow from the television.

"What're you watching?" I asked, but she didn't reply.

Joany went upstairs, then came half way back down and tossed me a blanket. In the morning, Lance roused me and drove us to school.

Next day Lance showed up at Camp Hero as it was getting dark and we didn't even play ball, just drove back to his house. Only this time I stopped him going up the stairs and asked what he was doing. He looked at me a minute with tired red eyes and shook his head.

"You're a breath of fresh air in this house," he said, and as he walked up the stairs I turned back to Joany sitting on the sofa. I walked toward her, slowly, like I was moving into a force field, and we sat in silence watching television—me just enjoying the feeling of her being close—till about twelve when Lance appeared, said he couldn't sleep, and drove me home.

Next afternoon in Montauk I didn't bother waiting for Lance and biked into the village and took the town bus to East Hampton, walking the rest of the way to Freetown, and saw him sitting on the porch, looking up at me like I was a total stranger. Like if I take you in to be with my sister fine, cause I took you, but on your own you better not even walk up my driveway.

Then Joany stepped out the door and walked right past us, headphones on, head tilted back toward the sky, wrapped in a scarf the color of her lips. I said her name, "Joany," but she just strolled on down the street.

"Well," I said to Lance, sitting there staring down, separating blades of grass on his palm, "guess I'll see where she's going."

"Do what you have to," he said.

"You're the one that brought me here," I said.

"I'm saying go ahead," Lance said, still looking down.

I saw Joany at the end of the road turn onto the sand and when I reached the bay, saw her out there standing on a jetty. Facing the water, she didn't see me come up behind her, but when I touched her shoulder she turned around, a serene half smile on her lips, her eyes squinting in the breeze, and I took her hand and we walked back and sat on the sand.

"Why don't you speak?" I said.

She smiled at me as if she were sorry.

"What is it?" I said. But she didn't answer.

"It's okay," I told her, releasing her hand, despite how warm it felt. "It's okay."

Joany took my hand back, held it in hers, and mouthed the words, "I know," then released my hand and turned back to the bay.

Back at the house, I found Lance still sitting on the porch.

"She been talking to you?" Lance said, and that was when I realized Joany didn't talk to him, or to anyone else either.

"What's she going to say to me?" I said.

"I don't know," he said. "You're supposed to be outside all this."

"Outside all what?"

"This," Lance said. "Family, Freetown."

"Maybe she needs to talk to someone on the inside," I said.

Lance huffed and shook his head.

"Whatever she needs," I said, "it's definitely not me," and I turned and headed back to town to get the bus.

Joany

Each afternoon I go for a long walk, away from the village and toward the bay, out onto Maidstone Beach. Lance says I spend too much time alone, but that's because he doesn't understand. Spends so much time worrying about me and about basketball, driving around and around, that when he finally comes home and sees me not talking, it only frustrates him more.

Then he brings home Ricky, like all that time out driving he'd been hunting for something, and he'd finally tracked it down and dragged it back to the house. And Ricky looked so, I don't know, not white so much as translucent, like he was there but not there.

So Lance leaves us downstairs alone, Ricky sitting in that chair watching movies with me through the night, and though I didn't know how long he'd stay, from the moment Ricky came into our house I knew Lance would be leaving.

Then I passed Ricky and Lance on the porch, on my way to the harbor. And I knew he would follow. Lance would sit and sink further and further into himself, or maybe drive around in circles, dreaming about leaving, and Ricky would come looking.

I wound my way along the narrow road and out onto Maidstone, onto the jetty jutting into the cold wind off the bay, just to stand there feeling myself enclosed by the wind . . . *Oh, hello Ricky* . . . not thinking of anything at all, just me and the water and sky . . . *Where's Lance, sitting on the porch or out driving his car in circles?*. . . releasing myself into the emptiness.

"Joany," Ricky said, his voice sounding like something heard from a thousand miles away, "I'm glad I found you."

You had no choice but to find me.

"Last night," he said, afraid to say the only thing he could say, "I wanted to stay with you."

My god, me, you wanted to stay with me, someone who wasn't even there.

He took my hand and we sat down and I just closed my eyes and waited for us not to do what we had never been going to do. But then he lets go my hand, like he knew it too, or didn't know it either, and I started feeling something, peace maybe, equilibrium, alone and not alone. When I opened my eyes Ricky was gone.

Lance

So Ricky comes back from the beach by himself, like that's it, nobody was measuring up.

"Where's Joany?" I asked him.

"How should I know?" Ricky said.

"You just left here there?"

"Nothing's happening with us, Lance."

"Don't say you didn't want it to," I said to him.

"It's what you wanted," he said. "You wanted me to whip you on the basketball court, now you want me to come in and help with your family, make it something it's not. Let's just say I was never here." And he walked on down the driveway, never looking back.

Then Joany came walking up from the other way, stopping right in front of me with a palm out toward my chest, her lips pursed, like they were permanently glued shut. Her eyes caught hold of mine and her lips pulled apart.

"What are you doing," Joany said, "sending him down there after me?"

"I thought you might speak to him," I said.

"What would I say?" Joany said. She took a step toward me, her lips again pursing, as if locking closed before once again opening. "What would I say, Lance?"

"I don't know," I said.

"We are not your wind up toys." She stood there glaring at me and began slowly shaking her head. "You need to get yourself going."

"What am I supposed to do?" I said. "Going away to college won't change anything. And what about you and Mommy?"

Joany's mouth tightened. "You think you're helping us, driving around in circles?"

"I'll get a job. With you talking, maybe we could—"

"Lance," Joany said, "you're going. You hear me? I'm talking now because someone needs to tell you: You're going."

I didn't go back out to Montauk until the spring, everything just starting to bloom. Must have been a weekend because the traffic on the highway was beginning to thicken with visitors. But when I reached the dirt drive and drove into the clearing before his house, I didn't see him on the court.

I walked over to knock on the door, but then I heard the rattle of the chain net and saw he'd appeared behind me—must have been there the whole time.

"Still at it, huh?" I said.

"Yup," Ricky said, shooting a lay-up. "How's Joany?"

"She's okay. Started talking right after you left."

"Glad to hear it," he said, but his tone was flat and I couldn't tell if he meant it. "How about you?" he asked. "Going to college?"

"I got a couple offers from D-2 schools. Decided on Clark up in Massachusetts."

Ricky switched to shoot with his left hand, flipping it off the board, catching it, and flipping it off the board.

"How about you?" I said.

"Might start working for my old man in the city. Might stay out here."

"Listen," I said, "all that stuff with my sister. I appreciate how you handled it."

"I didn't do anything," Ricky said, shooting the ball, catching it, shooting it.

"Maybe you just gave us a little time." I held out my hand. Ricky held the ball on his hip and we shook.

After a couple of steps toward my car, I turned back and gazed around at the open space, spreading out over the ocean, at the scattered trees beginning to bud, and took a last look at Ricky, catching the ball from the chain net, tossing the ball up the court and running off after it.